SIREN
Publishing

CW00506939

Ménage Everlasting

WEREWOLVES
OF
FOREVER, TEXAS

Her Wild Side

JANE JAMISON

Her Wild Side

Tasha Harden's mother has been bitten and transformed by the elusive vampire-like animal called a chupacabra. Tasha is determined to keep her mother alive when two mysterious men attempt to kill her. But first, she has to find her mother.

Werewolf brothers, Paul, Wick, and Shane Shilo have been watching the beautiful blonde for a while, unsure of what she's tracking. When she barrels into them as wolves, they can't resist her any longer. Talking her into trusting them isn't easy, though. She's suspicious even though she's drawn to them. However, the connection that brings all werewolves together is too strong for her to resist. They swear they'll help her find her mother, and she's grateful for the help.

Can they help Tasha find her mother in time? Even then, will Tasha accept them for what they are? Or will heartbreak break them apart?

Genre: Contemporary, Ménage a Trois/Quatre, Paranormal, Shape-shifter, Vampires/Werewolves
Length: 29,601 words

HER WILD SIDE

Werewolves of Forever, Texas 16

Jane Jamison

Siren Publishing, Inc.
www.SirenPublishing.com

A SIREN PUBLISHING BOOK

HER WILD SIDE
Copyright © 2018 by Jane Jamison

ISBN: 978-1-64243-022-6

First Publication: January 2018

Cover design by Les Byerley
All art and logo copyright © 2018 by Siren Publishing, Inc.

ALL RIGHTS RESERVED: This literary work may not be reproduced or transmitted in any form or by any means, including electronic or photographic reproduction, in whole or in part, without express written permission.

All characters and events in this book are fictitious. Any resemblance to actual persons living or dead is strictly coincidental.

WARNING: The unauthorized reproduction or distribution of this copyrighted work is illegal. Criminal copyright infringement, including infringement without monetary gain, is investigated by the FBI and is punishable by up to 5 years in federal prison and a fine of $250,000.

If you find a Siren-BookStrand e-book or print book being sold or shared illegally, please let us know at
legal@sirenbookstrand.com

PUBLISHER
Siren Publishing, Inc.
www.SirenPublishing.com

DEDICATION

Dear Reader,

Thank you for going on the journey of a lifetime with me. Writing is a solitary profession where the reward of an email from a reader saying that she/he enjoyed the book is worth more than the numbers on a paycheck. Without your continued support, I would spend my days wishing for what might have been.

Yours,
Jane Jamison

ABOUT THE AUTHOR

From an early age, Jane Jamison was fascinated with stories about werewolves, vampires, aliens, and whatever else might be hiding in her bedroom closet. To this day, she still swears she can hear growls and moans whenever the lights are out.

Born under the sign of Scorpio meant Jane was destined to be very sensual. Some would say she's downright sexual. Then one day she put her two favorite things together and found her life's true ambition: to be a romance author.

Jane spends each day locked in her office surrounded by her two furry bundles of joy and the heroes and heroines she loves. Her plans include taking care of her loving husband, traveling, and writing until her fingers fall off.

Jane also writes as Beverly Rae.

For all titles by Jane Jamison, please visit
www.bookstrand.com/jane-jamison

***For titles by Jane Jamison writing as
Beverly Rae, please visit***
www.bookstrand.com/beverly-rae

HER WILD SIDE

Werewolves of Forever, Texas 16

JANE JAMISON
Copyright © 2018

Chapter One

Tasha Harden was as nervous as a cat thrown into the middle of a dogfight. She hadn't seen her mother in over two years, and seeing her now was about to make Tasha lose her mind. She fiddled with her purse again as she had a thousand times before then slid out of her car, closed the door, and walked toward the café. Her limbs felt stiff, and her heart threatened to pound out of her chest. But this was something she needed to do. Not for her mother, but for herself.

Although she was thirty years old, Tasha suddenly felt like the fifteen-year-old girl her mother had left behind. Not legally or permanently—perhaps that would've been better—but the result had been the same. Tasha and her two brothers, Rick and John, may have grown up in their mother's house, but the woman who had acted as their mother had been their housekeeper. Rosita had been the one who'd given them care. Rosita had been the one who had wiped their tears away when they'd cried for their mother. Rosita had been the one they'd turned to whenever they'd wanted a mother's comfort. Her mother was soon relegated to a woman who called every few months and sent presents they didn't want. She could still hear her brothers' cries as they begged for their mother to come home. Every six months or so, her mother would show up, throw her arms around her children, and act as though she'd been away only a few days.

Her mother had always put her work first with her three children coming in a distant second. Most of the time, their father hadn't even registered on their mother's radar. As a scientist on the cutting edge of new and innovative digital technology, her mother was well known in corporate as well as scientific circles. Tasha couldn't say the same when it came to their family. She felt as though she didn't really know her mother at all.

Her father, having been hurt too many times by their mother, had sadly followed in his wife's footsteps and had also ended up going away all too often for work. At least he'd tried to leave the children with a relative who might care, but their Aunt Luanne had cared more about the contents of a Vodka bottle than she had for her niece and nephews.

Tasha put her hand on the doorknob of the café then paused. Noticing the tremble in her hand, she took her hand off the knob and crossed her arms, almost daring herself to go inside.

Why am I doing this? Why should I give a damn about her after all these years?

Yet as much as she wished she didn't, she still cared. She cared far more than her mother deserved.

No. That's not it at all. I'm curious, that's all. I don't really care. How can I? How can I care for the bitch that left us alone?

My mother's a bitch, all right.

She drew in a hard breath, hating that she'd thought of her mother as a bitch. Hating that she hated the fact that she'd called her mother a bitch.

If ever there was one…

Still, a child could never give up on her mother. Not even a mother who had given up on her child. Yet when Shirley Harden had called, Tasha had all too quickly agreed to meet. Hell, after her initial shock at hearing her mother's voice, she'd even found herself excited, eager to see her mother.

That excitement, however, hadn't lasted long. Not after the memories came flooding back.

Go on. Get it over with.

She didn't move.

Come on. I've done harder things than this.

Running her hand over the back of her neck and the stiffness growing there, she silently told herself to be strong, opened the door, and strode into the café, her head held high.

No matter what, I won't let her get to me. I'll listen to what she has to say, and then I'm gone. Once this is over, I can put her in the past once and for all.

"Honey, I'm over here."

Tasha's gaze jumped to the right of the café and found a striking woman sitting in a booth. Her mother was a thinner, mesmerizing version of Tasha. The short blonde hair, seemingly undimmed by age, was as vibrant as it always had been. The light brown eyes sparkled as though she hadn't aged a day in the past two years they'd been apart. Unlike Tasha's softer, "fluffier" body, her mother's body was firm and fit. She'd always been envious of her mother's athletic build, but her mother looked even better now.

Honey. What right does she have to still call me that? I haven't been her honey for a long time.

Her mother was smiling, but Tasha couldn't return the gesture. Instead, she stalked over to the booth then slid onto the seat. "Hello, Mother." Instantly, she wished she'd called her Shirley. She didn't deserve to be called "Mother."

Her mother's smile faded. "Can't you give your mother a hug?"

To her disgust, she wanted to do exactly that. Instead, she ignored the question and tried to turn her face into an unreadable mask. Tasha did her best to hold back her emotions. She had to be firm, resolute. If she didn't, her mother would wind her way back into her heart.

Get it over with.

"You wouldn't tell me on the phone, so tell me now. Why did you want to meet? Why now?" Did she sound petulant like a child who'd been denied ice cream for dessert?

Her mother gripped a napkin and began to tear it apart in little bits. The gesture, albeit small, gave Tasha a bit of satisfaction. At least her mother was nervous, too.

"So how are Rick and John? Are they all right?"

Tasha wasn't going to play the game. She wouldn't let her mother act as though she was still part of the family. She'd given up that privilege when she'd left them. Her brothers were the only family Tasha had. "They're fine." She held back the words "not that you really care."

Her mother opened her mouth to say something more then closed it. Obviously, she wanted to play the game of pretending that she was still their mother, but she'd caught on fast. If nothing else could be said of Shirley Harden, it was that she was an intelligent woman. "Fine. I see how it is. So let's get down to why we're here."

"Let's," said Tasha. She bit the inside of her mouth, keeping tears from burning her eyes. "Tell me why I'm here, Mother." *Damn it. I did it again.*

"At least you're still calling me mother."

Tasha bit back a retort, wanting to retract her words. "Just tell me what you want." She knew she was being harsh, but there was no other way. If she let her wall down, her mother would take advantage of her weakness.

"I won't go into the specifics about my work."

Shit. It's still all about her work.

Another napkin was shredded. Funny, she couldn't remember her mother being the nervous type. "Go on."

"I was in Africa doing research when it happened."

"I wouldn't think Africa would be on the cutting edge of technology." Tasha leaned back in her seat and placed her hands in her lap. Her mother had worked around the world, but most of her work had been centered in America. She rubbed her sweaty palms on her jeans.

"You'd be surprised what's going on there," said her mother. "But Africa doesn't include everything I need to tell you. It is, however, part of my story. Perhaps the most unbelievable part of it."

Although she didn't have anywhere else to go, Tasha looked at her watch, knowing her mother would understand the not-so-subtle hint. She wasn't sure how long she could stand being with her mother. "I haven't got all day."

Her mother nodded. "I was changed in Africa." Her light brown eyes, so much like Tasha's, lifted to hers. "While I was there, something attacked me."

As much as Tasha didn't want to, she couldn't help but be alarmed. "What do you mean something attacked you? Was it a lion? Something else? Someone else?" Her tone sounded stressed, as though she actually cared.

Damn it.

Her mother drew in a ragged breath. "Do you believe in mythical creatures?"

It took a moment for Tasha to regain her equilibrium. "What? Mythical creatures? What are you talking about? What does that have to do with anything?"

Her mother closed her eyes for a moment as though trying to gather her resolve. When she opened them again, Tasha could see the torment there.

"Have you ever heard of a creature called a chupacabra?"

"A what?"

"A chupacabra. Don't worry. I hadn't heard much about them, either. At least, not before this happened."

"What are they? And what do they have to do with you?" She didn't trust her mother, especially since nothing she'd said made sense. "I didn't come here to listen to a story about a mystical creature."

"Please humor me."

Tasha sat back and crossed her arms. "Fine. Go on."

"Thank you." Her mother continued to shred yet another napkin. "A chupacabra is thought to be something like a wild dog. It's supposed to be hairless with a pronounced spinal ridge. It's an ugly creature that supposedly sucks the blood from its prey."

Irritation flashed through Tasha. What the hell was her mother trying to do? Did she really think she'd buy into stupid shit like imaginary animals? "What's the point of this ridiculous story? Mother, if you don't start telling me why we're really here, I'm going to leave."

"No, please stay."

Her mother reached out to her and placed her hand over Tasha's. For a brief second, Tasha felt the thrill of having her mother touch her again. Quickly, she rejected the wonderful feeling and jerked her hand away.

"Then tell me the damn truth." Her mother had abandoned them as surely as though she'd walked out the door and gone forever, but she'd never lied to them. Why was she starting now?

"I know this is too incredible to believe. Sometimes, even now, I have a difficult time believing it happened. But what I'm about to tell you is the God's honest truth."

Tasha couldn't think of anything to say. How was she supposed to respond?

"While I was in Africa, I was attacked by a chupacabra. I didn't realize it until later, but it changed me that night."

Tasha snorted her derision. "I'd think getting attacked by mythical creature would change you." Sarcasm laced her tone. "But if you're asking me to believe that one of these things attacked you, then you're sadly mistaken. In fact, if you're going to insult my intelligence, I'm out of here."

Once again, her mother grabbed her hand, keeping her there. "Please. I'm telling you the truth. That thing bit me and changed me." Her mother took her hand away before Tasha could yank hers back.

"Now I'm one of them."

Had her mother gone insane? Had the stress of her work finally driven her over the edge?

"You're one of them?" It wasn't a serious question. She wasn't sure why she'd bothered asking. How could she dignify her mother's outrageous claim?

"Yes. I am."

Tasha arched an eyebrow. What was her mother trying to do? Plead temporary insanity? Pull on Tasha's heartstrings for forgiveness?

"I know it's difficult to comprehend."

"You think?" Tasha didn't hold back her derisive snort.

"I can show you if you want." Her mother's gaze scanned the room. "But not here. Not in front of others."

"Well, of course not. We wouldn't want anyone calling animal control, would we?" Irritation was beginning to grow into anger. "I'm assuming you've gotten your shots, right?"

Her mother sighed as though Tasha was letting her down. Then again, she was used to her mother's disappointment. Tasha had never been smart enough, clever enough, or pretty enough for her mother. At least now the disappointment was mutual.

"I understand how difficult this is for you. I wouldn't believe me, either."

"Oh, thanks. I'm so glad you understand." Tasha gritted her teeth and rubbed her hands over her jeans.

Her mother turned to dig in her purse. She brought out a small box that looked a lot like a walkie-talkie and slid it across the table to Tasha. "Please. Take this."

Tasha didn't want to touch the thing. Yet she couldn't resist. It was a simple device with only a few controls. "What is it?"

"It's a tracking device." Her mother laid her arm on top of the table, turning it so that Tasha could see the inside of her forearm. A small scar ran down the center of her flesh. "I inserted a tracking module in my arm. You can track me using that device." Suddenly, she tore the napkin in half, seeming even more nervous than before. "I want you to find me in case they—never mind." Her mother stopped abruptly, then made a feeble attempt to smile.

Had her mother actually gone crazy? She stared at the small scar. "What the hell did you do? Are you out of your mind? Why would you do that to yourself?"

"I want you to be able to find my body."

Tasha couldn't take her attention off the scar. "Why the hell would you put something under your skin? And why would I have to find your body? What's going on?"

Her mother pulled her arm back and, once again, began tearing up another napkin. "Did you know that chupacabras are supposed to live in Texas? That some people around the state have seen them?"

Tasha looked at the tracking device, then to her mother's arm, then up to meet her gaze. "Is that why you're back in Texas? Because you think there are others like you? Do you think other people have been attacked and changed into those things?"

"Tasha, please—"

But anger had pushed her past simple irritation. "What are you planning on doing, Mother? Are you planning on starting your own chupacabra pack? Or is there already a local chapter you can run?" Venom dripped from her tone. "This whole thing is ridiculous."

"I'm telling you the truth. You have to believe me. Honey, you know I've never lied to you and I'm not lying now."

"This is pure bullshit." *But she's right. She's never lied to me before.*

"You believe me. I can see it in your eyes."

"No." *And yet?* She laughed her mirthless sound even as she fought against believing. "Shit. You've got me acting like this is real."

Is insanity contagious?

"Please, honey, even if you don't want to believe me, take the tracking device. Please. I want to know that if—when—something happens to me that you'll find my body. That maybe, just maybe, you'll give me a proper burial." She lowered her chin, her gaze going to the table. "I know I wasn't much of a mother to you or your brothers, but I'm asking you to do this one last thing for me."

"This is insane." Was she just as crazy to pick up the device and put it into her purse? Yet, she couldn't find it in her to turn her mother down. "I'll take it, but only because I don't want to argue."

"As long as you have it, then I'm good. You'll be able to pick up my signal from miles away."

"I don't believe I'm asking this, but who is the *they* you're talking about, Mother? Are you in some kind of trouble?" At least, that was something she could understand. Her mother's work dealt in very confidential information. She'd often wondered if her mother's work could be considered dangerous.

Her mother ignored her questions. "Thank you, honey. Just know that I'm going to be going a remote area of the state. I need to…get away."

"You're talking about disappearing, aren't you? Into the middle of nowhere? Come on, Mother. You're not the type to be without a five-star restaurant nearby."

"I'm different now, but—" Her mother's gaze slid over Tasha's shoulder to the door beyond. Her face paled. "I have to go now," said her mother in a harried voice. She grabbed her purse and slid out of the booth.

"But where exactly are you going? You can't just throw this shit on me and then leave. Tell me what's going on? Is someone threatening you?" She hurried to follow as her mother dashed away, not to the front door but toward the rear the building. "Where the hell are you going?"

Her mother glanced back once. "Don't follow me." She paused long enough to turn back. Her fearful gaze met hers. "If you don't hear from me in a week or two, use the tracking device. Go northwest toward a town called Forever. I won't be in the town, but close by." Her gaze slipped behind Tasha, and her eyes widened. "I have to go now."

"Where are you going? What's in Forever? Who are you running from?" She'd never heard of the town. But then again, there were a lot of small towns in Texas that never made it on a map, much less known to everyone in the state.

Her mother pushed through the rear door and ran out into the alley. By the time Tasha made it to the door and shoved it wide open, her mother looked back again then disappeared around the side of the dumpster. She couldn't think of anything else, any other way to keep her mother from leaving, so she shouted, "Show me. You said you'd show me."

Her mother's voice came from behind the Dumpster. "Two weeks, then find me."

"Damn it. Show me or I'm not doing a fucking thing." She wondered if her mother would chastise her for cussing. Her criticism was one of the few things Tasha remembered about her. "If you want me to believe this bullshit, you have to show me."

Surely, that'll put an end to this nonsense. Checkmate, Mother.

Tasha had so many unanswered questions swirling around, but they were all lost as her mother stepped out from behind the Dumpster. Tasha narrowed her eyes, unbelieving what she was seeing.

Her mother's body began to change. Clothes tore apart as limbs broke. In shock, Tasha stayed where she was, unable to move as her mother fell to all fours. Within a minute, a canine-like creature with sharp spines running down its back lifted its head and growled.

The creature was exactly as her mother had described it. Deadly fangs and claws broke through flesh. Hair was lost, fading away to a strange leathery skin. It crouched, ready to attack.

Tasha fell against the wall, too stunned to stay upright. Everything inside her told her to run, but she had no strength. Instead, she slumped to a sitting position.

The creature that had been her mother advanced on her slowly. Red eyes blazed at her as it opened its mouth to bite. Saliva dripped from its jaws.

Mother? Oh, God. Mother.

"There it is."

Tasha couldn't take her eyes off the creature until the creature turned its blazing eyes toward the entrance of the alley. Two figures hidden in the darkness stood at the entrance. With a growl, her mother spun around and dashed out the other side of the alley.

Tasha remained where she was, unable to move, unable to help her mother. Would they help? Or would they do to her what they'd probably wanted to do to her mother? The questions remained unanswered as they hurried away.

* * * *

One week later

Tasha checked the tranquilizer gun one last time. She'd become obsessive about making sure the rifle was ready to use. Fortunately, she'd come to shooting naturally and had required very little instruction on how to use the weapon. As she slid into the seat of the ATV, she placed the rifle in its holder.

Maybe tonight is the night.

She hadn't waited the two weeks as her mother had asked. Not after seeing those two figures in the darkness. She had no doubt that they'd been after her mother. No matter what she thought of her mother, no matter how complicated her feelings were, she couldn't let them hurt her. Instead, she'd left town the very next day, using the tracking device to pick up her mother's signal.

Still, she didn't doubt the effectiveness of the device. If her mother said it would work, then it would. Yet, initially, she'd wondered if the unit had malfunctioned when the trail had crisscrossed the Texas landscape. At last, she'd finally ended up closer to Forever. But why had it taken her mother so long to get there? Why her mother told her to go to the small town if she hadn't intended on going directly there was still a mystery. Had she been trying to get away from someone else? Had she done her best to hide her destination? Or had she simply changed her mind several times?

So far, Tasha hadn't actually gone into the small town of Forever. Why should she? What was she supposed to do? Ask the people if they'd seen a chupacabra in the area? If she had, she wouldn't have blamed them if they'd run her off. Instead, she'd stayed in the area, living in the small cramped camper she pulled behind a rented pickup. Taking time off from her job as a social worker hadn't been easy, but because of her exemplary work record, her boss had said he'd cover for her. At least, for a while. But the time she'd been allowed to take off was quickly coming to an end. If she didn't find her mother soon, she didn't know what she'd do.

Could she leave and forget about her mother? Or would she regret not abandoning her mother for the rest of her life?

Damn it. She *abandoned us. Why shouldn't I do the same to her?*

And yet, she couldn't.

Riding across the Texas landscape at night was a foolish thing to do, but from the research she'd done on the chupacabra creature, she knew her chances of finding her mother at night were better. The ATV's engine roared underneath her as she pressed her foot against the gas pedal. Every so often, she'd glance down at the tracking device and check on the blimp that marked her mother's whereabouts. Excitement filled her as she saw the blimp blinking faster and faster.

I'm getting close. Closer than I've been before.

Once she'd found her mother, she wasn't sure what to do. She only knew that she had to find her before those two men found her first.

Would she take her mother home with her? Or would her mother refuse and run off again? Would her mother still be in danger at home? And even if she wasn't, was there a cure? Would her mother know of others that might help? But if she'd had a solution, why hadn't she sought their help? Who was tracking her? And why?

The questions came again as they had so many times before. She'd find the answers, someway, somehow, but for now, all that mattered was finding her mother.

The vehicle flew over the ground, lifting into the air with every leap over the next rise. She held tightly to the handlebars, but refused to slow down, no matter how dangerous it was. Another glance at the tracking device proved she was gaining ground.

She resisted the urge to check around her. If the two men were close by, she wasn't sure what she could do to stop them. The only weapon she had was the tranquilizer gun. If they were armed, how could she defend herself, much less her mother, against them?

A dark form dashed across the path. Her heart leapt into her throat, and she pressed harder on the gas. Revving the motor, she took after what she hoped was her mother.

Again, the dark form rushed past her and down the gravel path. How had her mother circled back on her? Suddenly, the animal turned a sharp right and disappeared again.

No, I won't let you get away.

She turned the corner going at breakneck speed. As soon as she did, she knew she was in trouble. As the ATV balanced on two wheels, threatening to tip over, she saw the three animals in the middle of the road. She slammed on the brakes, throwing up dirt and gravel. Her breath caught in her throat until the ATV landed again on four wheels and skidded to a stop.

What the hell?

She'd been searching for her mother, but it wasn't her mother that stood in front of her. Three huge wolves barred the path. They stood side by side, almost as though they were intentionally forming a barrier.

Each was equally as broad, equally as huge as the others. Amber eyes stared at her, yet she felt no animosity in them. One was black, one brown, and the other more of a golden color. The ears were laid forward, a friendly gesture by canine standards. Their tails weren't hung between their legs, but held upright as though in greeting. Yet they were wolves, predators of the night.

A strange sensation shook her, swiftly searing through her body. Instead of fear, she felt suddenly more alive than she'd ever had. She was drawn to them as though she'd known them all of her life.

For a moment, she actually considered getting out the ATV and walking over to touch them. Fortunately, she came to her senses.

She shook herself mentally and reached for her gun. Not that she could take all of them with one shot. But maybe, just maybe, one shot would be enough to scare them off. "Get out of here," she said in a voice as firm as she could. If she couldn't shoot all of them, then, hopefully, she could at least pretend to be in command. "Get out of here," she repeated.

Surprisingly, she wasn't afraid of them. Furthermore, she could see that they weren't afraid of her. They stood their ground, not moving forward, yet not leaving, either. She glanced around quickly, unwilling to take her eyes off them for too long. But now that they'd blocked her way, had she lost track of her mother? One look at the tracking device told her she had.

Damn it. How'd she get out of range so fast?

But worrying about her mother would have to wait. She had to deal with the danger at hand.

The wolves returned her stare. It seemed that they were at a stalemate.

"Okay, nice wolves, let's just pretend we didn't see each other." She kept her voice as soothing as possible.

Slowly, she reversed gears in the ATV and began to back up. The wolves didn't move. Did she dare turn the ATV around and put her back to them? Yet she had no choice. She couldn't back up all the way down the trail. Putting the vehicle into drive, she pressed on the gas and turned the wheel as hard as she could. Growls lifted onto the air as fear finally locked onto her. Straightening the wheels, she drove as fast as she could back the way she came.

She'd never seen one before, at least not in real life, but she knew these wolves were larger than most. Yet it wasn't their size that had made them seem…different. They had an unusual manner about them, an almost a human-like presence.

Hunting my mother is starting to get to me.

Yet, as she pulled up to her camper, turned off the ATV's engine, and checked around to make sure they hadn't followed her, she knew it wasn't the duration of the hunt that had made the wolves seem different. Those wolves weren't ordinary wolves. They were somehow more. So much more.

But what?

Chapter Two

Paul Shiloh raced after the beautiful girl on the ATV. His brothers, Shane and Wick, ran by his side. After watching the woman for a few days, wondering what she was tracking, they'd decided to gain more information. With every day that passed, they'd dared to get closer to her. Then, once she'd begun heading down the path while going far too fast, they'd decided they had to keep her from hurting herself. She was lucky she hadn't overturned the vehicle when she'd taken it around the corner on two wheels.

They hid in the shadows as she parked the ATV, glanced around, obviously wary of her surroundings. Her eyes widened in the same moment he felt the magical sensation hit him. Thrilled, he almost gave them away as he danced on his paws, eager to take her for his own. He'd never experienced the connection before seeing her a few days earlier, but he had no doubt that the feeling was real. Even if he hadn't heard others describing the how they'd felt, he would've recognized it for what it was. What else could the electrical, stimulating sensation be except the invisible bond that flowed between a werewolf and his mate?

Once they were sure she was safely inside the camper, they ran back to their ranch house and shifted as soon as he was inside. Although he tried to remain casual, his excitement continued to grow. He was more certain than ever as he pulled on his clothes.

Beer in hand, Paul sat down on the couch, eager to talk. "Do either of you have any doubts?" As if he had to ask. They'd felt the connection with her the first moment they'd laid eyes on her. Keeping away from her, keeping their beasts in check had been the hardest things he'd ever done. But there was a mystery about her, and they had to know what was going on before they approached her.

Wick shoved a shock of dark brown hair away from his eyes. "No doubt as far as I'm concerned. She's the one, all right." His ever-ready grin came, lighting his face. "She's our mate. God help her."

Paul grinned at his brother. Wick was the humorous one of the trio. As the middle brother, Wick wasn't as serious as Paul was or as quiet as Shane. "So what are we going to do? Isn't it time?"

Shane was on his feet, pacing the room back and forth. He turned and confronted them. "Hell yeah, it's time. If we wait any longer, she might light out and we'll never see her again."

Wick was already striding toward the door as he spoke. "I said I don't have any doubt now. Never really did." He paused at the door, his hand on the knob. "Get moving. I'll drive."

Paul wasn't about to be left behind as they piled into the truck and headed for the camper. The terrain was rough, jostling them. She could've easily torn up her truck and camper going over the pot-holed dirt road. She must've been searching for a way into the pasture and gotten lucky to find the road. Even they didn't travel it often. But how she'd gotten there no longer mattered. *She* was all that mattered now.

He wasn't sure what they'd say once they got there. But whatever came out, however it came out, they'd get to know her better.

Still undecided on what to say, he was the first one out of the pickup when they pulled up next to her camper. The lights were on, showing she was at home. Questions swirled. What kind of woman came out into the middle of nowhere in a camper? What kind of woman hunted in the dark? And what was she hunting for? So far, they hadn't seen anything since they'd been so intent on watching her. Tonight, however, he knew she'd seen something. Judging from the way she'd driven the ATV, she'd been hell-bent on catching it. Obviously, she'd finally found her prey.

They stood outside the camper for a moment and studied each other. This was the moment they'd been waiting for almost all their lives. This was the moment they'd finally meet their mate.

Let's do this. Now.

Paul couldn't stand it any longer. He nodded then lifted his hand, fisted it, and banged against the door. He hadn't meant to hit it so hard, but his enthusiasm had overtaken him.

"Take it easy, bro," said Shane. "We don't want to scare her off."

"Which means we don't tell her what we are right away," added Wick.

"Maybe we should wait until tomorrow? During the day?"

Paul joined Shane in giving Wick a "what the fuck" stare? No way could he wait a second longer.

Besides, hadn't they already discussed all of this? Now wasn't the time to start changing their plans. "I've already knocked. Just let me take the lead." He knocked again, this time a little lighter, yet still forcefully. Even now, with the door between them, he could feel the connection. He could sense her presence and know that she was so close by.

He had so much he wanted to tell her. So much he wanted to share with her. Not only his ranch but his heart. He wanted to let her know that they were her mates. For so many years, he'd practiced what he would say, yet when she opened the door, rifle in hand, he was suddenly at a loss for words.

Although he'd seen her on her ATV, her golden hair flying out behind her as she raced down the trails, he'd never realized just how beautiful she was. Long, blonde hair streamed around her shoulders like a golden waterfall. Her full breasts pushed at her T-shirt. The light in the camper behind her floated around her, making her seem like a goddess descending from the sun. She was curvy in all the right places, and his mouth watered thinking about how his tongue would skim over her flesh. Some people would say she was too heavy, but as far as he was concerned, she was the perfect size. He checked with his brothers. Judging by their hungry looks, she was the perfect size for them, too.

She lifted the rifle just enough to prove a point. "Who are you? What are you doing here?"

Her voice, albeit tinged with fear, was like a song sung by the birds in the trees. There was a melodic lilt to it that dove down into him, grabbed hold of his heart, and wouldn't let go. It wasn't until Wick nudged him in the ribs that he remembered he was the one who was supposed to talk.

He adopted his most charming smile and stuck out his hand. "Name's Paul Shiloh. This one"—he jerked his head toward Wick— "is my brother Wick. The other one is my youngest brother, Shane. Wick's thirty, and Shane is twenty-eight." He didn't need to see his brothers' expressions to know that he sounded like an idiot. He was rambling. But what did they expect when a man spoke to his mate for the first time?

She frowned and, for a moment, he saw recognition in her eyes. Taking short sniffs, he could smell the sexual attraction on her. She was already getting hot and heavy for them, and she didn't realize why. But he knew why. She was sensing the connection, too.

Then she seemed to shake it off. "I don't care who you are. I don't know what you're doing here. And I want you to leave." She jerked the barrel of the rifle at them. "Now."

"We don't mean you any harm." He didn't get the impression that she was afraid of them, but that she was simply leery, cautious, like any sensible woman would be. "It's just that we were wondering what you're doing parked on our land." Totally not what he'd planned to say, but there it was.

She blinked, obviously caught off-guard. "This is your land?"

"That's right. This is the Broken Bone Ranch. This is our ranch, and you're squatting on it." Inwardly, he cringed. What was he saying? Why was he challenging her? At the very least, he wished he hadn't sounded so harsh, much less accused her of doing something illegal.

Shane let out a low growl, so low Paul doubted she could've heard it. It was a warning to Paul to watch his words. "Not that we mind. Still, we'd kind of like to know why people are taking up space on our land." Shit. He wasn't doing any better. She'd rattled him, making him keep babbling like an idiot.

"Are you running me off?" Her voice held a hint of worry.

And the verbal diarrhea kept coming. "You had to have known someone owned the land. Still, you didn't bother checking. Why?"

Any hint of worry was gone in the combative glint in her eyes. "I didn't have time to ask. So? Are you running me off or not?"

He wondered how feisty she could get. She had to be brave to have come out in the middle of nowhere by herself. At least, they'd assumed she was by herself. So far, they hadn't seen anybody with her.

Damn it, I hope she doesn't have a boyfriend. Or, worse, a husband.

He and his brothers had talked about the possibility of their mate being with another man. Worse, a fiancé. Or, even more horrible, a husband. They hadn't liked to think about it, but they'd come to the conclusion that if she was already involved, then they'd still tell her who they were and that she was their mate. She'd have to make the decision to either go back to her current man or stay with them. Would she choose to leave? Or would the connection urge her to leave him for them? He sure hoped so. If not, he'd live a long, lonely life.

Damn. Don't let her have a child, either.

If she and her man shared a child, then it would be a different matter. For the sake of the child, they'd back off without telling her about them. They'd commit themselves to a life of misery without her. His gaze jumped behind her, searching for someone else in the camper. He almost sighed out loud when he didn't see anyone.

"Are you still taking the lead?" asked Wick. "Because if you are, you're doing a piss poor job of it."

"Answer her question, man," urged Shane.

Paul met her gaze and almost couldn't manage to get the words out. "No. We're not asking you to leave. We'd never ask you to leave."

"Then why are you here? And how did you know I was on your land?" At last, she cradled the rifle instead of keeping it pointed at them. Her eyes narrowed. "Have you been spying on me?"

His first impulse was to admit it. Thankfully, he ignored that impulse. "Of course not. We just happened by and saw the camper."

Shit. What the hell is wrong with me?

"You three were just wondering around? Out here?"

"Yeah. Sure." He tried to act as though what he'd said was the most natural answer in the world.

She didn't believe him. He could see the suspicion in her eyes. Besides, he'd been told often enough that he was a lousy liar.

"Okay. Fine. But if you're not kicking me off the land, I have things I need to do."

He couldn't let her shut the door. Not yet. He couldn't bring himself to not bask in the glow of her beautiful face a little longer. He flattened his palm against the door, keeping her from closing it. Fear splintered across her face then was followed quickly by anger. She repositioned the rifle again, pointing the muzzle directly at him.

"Take it easy. Like I said, we don't mean you any harm."

"Then you'll let me close the door."

She was beautiful when she was angry. Her oval face, rounded and soft, tightened. Her full lips narrowed into a line. "Still, it's not safe for a woman to be out here all by herself. You are all by yourself, aren't you?" Could he get any more obvious? But then, he didn't care as long as her answer was the one he hoped to hear.

She hesitated before nodding. "I am. But that doesn't mean I can't take care of myself."

Wick chuckled. "I don't doubt that one damn bit."

Shane put his arm around Paul's shoulder. "What my older brother is trying to get at is this. It'd be a lot safer for you to park your camper closer to our house. In fact, we have an extra bedroom you could use. And a nice hot shower, too."

"Not to mention a good breakfast the morning." Paul heard Wick snort. Not that he could blame his brother. Paul had never made breakfast for anyone except himself. Shane was the cook in the family. Even then, that wasn't saying much.

She relaxed—a little. "Thanks, but I'm fine just where I am."

"You never told us why you're here," said Paul. They'd figured out that she was chasing something, but that something was still unknown. "And you never told us your name."

The corners of her mouth lifted upward. "No. I didn't."

Yet she wanted to tell them. He could sense her warming to them. But what could've brought her to Forever? Not that he'd seen her in town and he hadn't heard of any visitors, either. Had the connection truly brought her to them? Or was it merely a coincidence that they'd found each other? Whatever the reason, the connection was there and growing stronger by the minute.

"Oh, so you're a woman of mystery," added Shane.

Her gaze scanned his brother. From the way she slid her tongue over her lips, she liked what she saw. "No mystery. I'm just a private person is all. Thanks for stopping by, but good night."

Once again, she started to close the door. And once again, he stopped her. "Aw, come on. You know you want to take us up on our offer. What woman would want to sleep in a camper when she could sleep in a soft bed?" He made an *X* over his heart. "You have my word. We won't bother you."

Unless you want us to.

He could sense his brothers' wolves rising to the surface. He could sense their need growing as strong as his. If they let their wolves have their way, they wouldn't care what she had to say. They'd take their mate as wolves had always done in the past. But the men they were wouldn't take a woman that way. Not against her will. No matter how much they wanted her. No matter how much his cock was beginning to stiffen.

Once again, she shook her head. Thankfully, her focus stayed on his face. "No, thank you. I'm perfectly happy where I am. If it's still okay with you for me to stay here. It's okay, right?"

He got the impression that she wanted him to keep asking her to stay closer to their house. Perhaps she knew she'd feel safer, but was too proud to back down. So he asked again. "Look, I can understand why you wouldn't want to stay in the same house with three strange men, but it only makes sense for you to move your camper closer. That way you'll still have your privacy, but you'll have access to more creature comforts." He smiled, trying to coax her more. "Plus, we'll sleep easier knowing you're safe."

She was thinking about it. Her hesitancy said as much. At last, she relented. "Well, I guess since you're allowing me to stay on your land it's only fair that I should do as you ask. But if I move closer to your home, you promise to respect my desire to be left alone?" She narrowed her eyes. "No means no in every way and in every thing."

"Absolutely," interjected Wick a little too enthusiastically.

"We'll help you get everything moved, too," added Shane. "Give us the keys and we'll load the ATV in the back of the truck right now."

She took a while to answer, giving Paul hope. "Okay. I'll move closer to your home. Unless it's far away. I need to be in this area."

Why? What are you searching for?

But Paul didn't dare ask. Not when she'd just agreed to park her camper close to their home. Pushing her wouldn't be wise. Still, he had to hold back a big grin. "It's not that far. We'll get you there in no time. Once we get you set up by the house, we can even feed you a little dinner. How's that sound?"

He knew he'd made a mistake as soon as she started shaking her head. "No, no. I don't want any dinner. I just want to be left alone. If you can't leave me be, then I'm staying right where I am."

Shane whacked him in the arm. "Don't pay attention to him. We'll stick by what we promised."

Paul's neck stiffened as he waited for her response. If he'd blown it by offering her dinner, he'd catch hell from his brothers. The thing was, if he'd blown it, he deserved to catch hell. "There's only one thing you have to do."

She cast him a suspicious look. "What's that?"

"Tell us your name."

She pulled in a long breath, apparently relieved. "I'm Tasha Harden."

"It's good to meet you, Tasha Harden." *Real good.* "So? Are we moving you or what?"

Again, she took her time to answer then finally relented. "Fine. I'll get things ready to roll inside while you guys handle my ATV." She snatched up the set of keys off a nearby table and tossed them to Shane. "Load 'em up, boys." Then, with a grin that might have stilled Paul's heart from the brilliance, she closed the door.

* * * *

Tasha eased the curtain aside on the camper's window enough to peek out. The lights were still on in the men's house, most of them on in the second-story rooms, but it was still early yet. Groaning, she turned the curtain loose and forced herself away from the window.

True to their word, they'd moved her camper closer to their house and had then left her alone. She'd sat in the camper for a while, wondering about them. Worse, she'd sat in her camper, wishing they'd break their promise to give her privacy.

Had she made a mistake by accepting their offer? She still couldn't believe she'd taken them up on it. Yet, as soon as she'd opened the door, she'd felt a compulsion to make them happy, to please them in any way she could. The feeling was similar to the way she'd felt when she'd seen the three wolves, except there was an underlining sexual tension. She'd been attracted to men before, but she'd never wanted to rip any man's clothes off and take him as soon as she'd met him. She'd never hungered for a man without him saying a word. But she had for these men. It had taken everything in her power not to put the gun down and invite them inside.

What was it about them? They were different in that they were the best-looking men she'd ever seen, but that wasn't the reason. Their broad shoulders, strong arms, and powerful legs weren't the main reason she'd accepted their offer. Not even their thick hair and glistening eyes were responsible. No, it was the way in which they'd held themselves. As though they commanded the entire world. They were more than confident. They were mesmerizing men who should be immortalized on monuments. Silently, inexplicably, she'd known they exuded a knowledge that few men possessed. Sure, she found them attractive, but more, she found them almost irresistible.

Almost irresistible was scary as hell.

Which is why she should've turned down their invitation. If she'd spent any more time with them, they *almost* would've gone away. Even now, she paced back and forth in her small camper, fighting the urge to go into the house and beg them to take her.

She had to keep herself in check. She hadn't come to find men. She'd come trying to find her mother. Until she did, she couldn't let herself be distracted, no matter how sexually compelling these men were.

She had to do something to get her mind off the men. If she didn't, she was bound to do something she'd regret. Grabbing a bottle of wine, she poured herself a stiff drink, then downed half the glass.

Something I'd regret? How could any woman regret having those men between her legs?

She took another drink, this time straight from the bottle. Flopping down on the small bench-like seat, she glared at the door and willed herself not to open it.

What the hell is wrong with you? Think about your mother.

Yet images of the men came back, like fantasy men from her

dreams. Another drink followed the last until she realized she'd consumed half the bottle. Her head swam, her sight growing blurry.

Shit and double shit. What have I gotten myself into?

* * * *

"You really didn't need to do this." Tasha surveyed the spread of food on the kitchen table. When Shane had shown up earlier, she hadn't been able to turn down the offer to have breakfast with the men. She was hungry, yes, but she was hungry for more than food. But it would only be food that she'd have this morning. At least, that was what she kept telling herself.

Shane waved her into a chair. "This is what we do every morning." He looked at the scrambled eggs, bacon, sausage, toast, and hash browns as though trying to understand what she thought was unusual.

"You eat all of this every morning?" Her gaze scanned over the men, taking in their shredded bodies. "How do you keep in shape? If I ate like this every morning, I'd be as big as a house."

I am as big as a house. *At least a small one.*

As though he could read her mind, Wick offered her a plate then handed her the bowl filled with scrambled eggs. "First off, you're perfect exactly the way you are. Secondly, it wouldn't matter what size you were. You'll always be beautiful."

It was tough to decide which one she loved more at that moment. The aroma of delicious eggs or the delicious man standing next to her? Unable to say thanks, she smiled it instead. "This really smells great. So who did all this cooking?"

Paul took a seat next to hers and began loading up his plate. He piled food on top of food, and she wondered how any one person could eat all of it. "That would be Shane. What he doesn't cook well, he makes up for in quantity. We have big appetites. Go on. Don't be like all those other girls. Eat everything you want. We like a woman who knows how to chow down."

Could she ask for anything better? Three handsome-as-hell men who want to see her eat? Were they normal? Or did they have some kind of food fetish?

Still, she took him at his word and motioned for him to pass the hash browns. "I'm sorry I was less than friendly last night. It's just that, you know, a woman alone and all that."

Shane plopped yet another bowl of food, this time a plate of fried potatoes, onto the table. "Don't worry about it. We're just glad you decided to move your camper. We wouldn't have felt right leaving you out there alone."

"Why? Is Forever a dangerous place?" She hadn't expected a scary answer, but when they didn't answer straight away, it threw her. "It's not, is it?"

"No," answered Wick. "But then again, is any place in the world perfectly safe?"

He had a point. Still, was he holding something back?

Paul swallowed a big helping of food. "How about you tell us why you're out here now. Don't take this the wrong way, but you seem like a city girl. You don't strike us as the kind of girl that would go camping by herself in the middle of nowhere."

She shouldn't have accepted their offer of breakfast. She should've known the questions would accompany the food. "Like I said last night, my business is my business. I have my reasons for being here, and I don't think I need to spill my guts to all of you." She stuck her fork into the hash browns then slid them into her mouth. She almost groaned in ecstasy. If they didn't think Shane's cooking was terrific, then what would they think of her cooking?

She stopped chewing as realization struck her. *Why am I thinking about cooking for them?*

"But you have to admit that a woman out in the middle of nowhere all by her lonesome isn't being a very bright girl." Wick shrugged at Shane's glare. "I'm just saying what we're all thinking."

She took in a few more bites, keeping quiet and hoping they'd get the hint that she didn't want to talk any longer. At least, not about her safety. She'd moved closer to their home. For now, that was as far as she was willing to go. Yet as she reached for the glass of orange juice Shane had poured for her, she could tell they weren't the type to take hints.

"At the very least, you should have a gun with you. A regular gun. Not a tranq gun," stated Paul. "Plus, riding around on an ATV at night is dangerous. Hell, you almost—" He slammed his mouth shut, abruptly cutting off his sentence.

"First of all, I have a gun." It was a white lie, one that would suggest she had another gun besides the tranquilizer rifle. "Second of all, I almost what?" Once again, she wondered if they'd been spying on her.

"A tranquilizing gun isn't the kind of gun you need out here." Shane shoveled more food onto his plate. "You need something to put an animal down for good, not just asleep." He paused, his fork stuck in mid-air, his mouth parted. "I'm talking about shooting an animal if it attacks you. Not out of sport. You aren't hunting innocent animals, are you?"

Innocent animals? The phrase sounded strange, but she understood what he meant. Besides, what could she tell them? That she was hunting her mother? "No. I'm not out to shoot any innocent animals. And, like I told you last night, I can take care of myself."

She began eating faster, knowing she'd need to get out before the questions grew any more difficult to answer. Yet there it was again. The strange sensation she'd felt the night before. It had struck her as soon as she'd awakened and had grown stronger the moment she'd stepped into their house.

Somehow, she'd managed to convince herself that the sensation was a result of exhaustion or the excitement of meeting the men. But once she saw them again, she'd known it was something else, something more. She concentrated on the sensation, trying to understand it. She felt as though an electric eel had wrapped itself around her body and was sending currents through it. Yet, instead of being afraid, she found herself liking the feeling. Hell, even loving it. She didn't need to understand the how or why of it to know the sensation had something to do with the men. Every time she looked at them, the feeling grew stronger, urging her to throw caution to the wind and ask them to take her. No, more than that. To *beg* them to take her.

"Naw. You're hunting something all right. That much is obvious." Paul leaned over the table toward her. "But what? What kind of animal are you planning on hunting down and taking alive?"

Suddenly, her appetite was gone. Although the sensation made her feel connected to them, drawn to them, their questions were making her uncomfortable. When would they stop asking questions? When would she have answers to her own questions? What if she gave into the sensation? Would offering herself to them make them shut up? Would indulging in the urge to have them make the feeling go away?

"We're only trying to keep you safe. You know that, right?" asked Wick.

She met his gaze and wondered if they truly cared. Or were they only worried about the liability of her getting hurt while on their land? Strangely, she thought they did care. Did they feel something, too? Were they picking up on the strange vibe between them? Yet, if they had, why hadn't they made a move?

She stood, suddenly needing to get away. They stood seconds later, ready to stop her. She held up her hands, palms out, warding them off. "This was a mistake." Whether she meant coming to breakfast or staying close to the house, even she wasn't sure. "Thank you for breakfast, but I have to go."

"Tasha, don't run off." Shane was by her side faster than she'd have thought possible. "We promise not to ask any more questions. Stay. Eat. We'll talk about whatever you want to. Or nothing at all."

"No." She shook her head even as she fought the compulsion to snag him by his shirt and tug his lips to hers. "This was a mistake," she repeated. Fearing what she might do more than their reactions, she whirled around and rushed out of the house.

She knew they'd follow her. And, oddly, a part of her wanted them to. Yet instead of heading to her camper, she hopped on her ATV. Whichever man had taken it off the truck had left the keys in the ignition. With one glance back at them, she revved up the engine and took off.

* * * *

"Damn, guys, we sure fucked the hell out of that." Not only was Wick angry at his brothers, he was angry at himself, too. They should've let her eat breakfast in peace. Instead, they'd pushed her too hard.

"Shut the hell up," warned Paul.

"Hey, you two, there's no use going at each other's throats." Shane ran a hand through his hair. "We need to figure this out. She's hunting, but she's not about to tell us what for. Our main priority now is to keep her safe until she feels comfortable enough to tell us what's going on."

"Fuck. This isn't going down like it should." Wick stalked toward their pickup then stalled. "Damn it. There's no use taking off after her. She'd just get mad as hell about it." Yet the urge to chase after their mate was strong. They couldn't chase her as men, but should they chase her as wolves?

"You mean madder than she already is?" Paul glanced at the truck, probably thinking the same thing Wick was. "We don't have a choice. Even as wolves, we couldn't catch up with her now. Shit."

Wick let out a low growl, barely keeping his wolf from rising to the surface. They'd finally found their mate, but she was putting herself at risk. Yet, instead of going after her, instead of running with her to make certain she was safe, he had to keep his head. He had to think like a man, not like a wolf. "It's already tough going with her. What the hell's going to happen when she finds out what we are?"

Paul's eyes were flecked with amber, showing his wolf fighting to take control. "Maybe we should tie her up before we tell her?"

Wick lifted an eyebrow. "Seriously? You want to win her heart by treating her like a prisoner?"

Fangs peeked out from between his brother's lips. "No. Of course not. Still…" He let out a low, irritated grow. "But, damn it, we don't want her running off."

"Let's do this the right way. We figure out what she's doing, and then, once that part's settled, we tell her she's our mate. We give the connection between us time to work. *Then* we tell her what we are."

Wick couldn't help but laugh. "Yeah, that'll be easy."

"Maybe not easy, but well worth it," challenged Paul.

"And in the meantime, we have to hope she doesn't get hurt." For one of the very few times in his life, Wick felt helpless.

"Well, this fuckin' blows." Shane kicked his boot into the dirt.

What else could they do? "Yeah, bro. That about sums it up." It was a long shot, but it was their only chance. "Fuck this. I'm going after her. One way or another, I'll find her."

Chapter Three

The wind blew through Tasha's hair as she sped down the back road. She was upset, and she was angry, but it wasn't only because of what the men had said. More of her anger came from the fact that she couldn't deny that they were right. What business did she have riding around in the middle of nowhere? She'd taken a crash course on learning to drive the ATV. Then another hurried lesson on learning to shoot the tranquilizer gun. If statistics were correct, she'd end up shooting herself or someone else instead of her mother. Plus, she couldn't deny that she didn't know much about being in the wilderness. She was a city girl just as the men had said. What little she knew about hunting and camping came from her research on the Internet.

But what was she supposed to do? Just pick up and leave her mother behind? Even though there was a huge rift between her and her mother, she couldn't make herself turn her back on her. How could she when there were people after her mother? Her mother had given her the tracking device for a reason. The reason she'd given had been for Tasha to find her body, but Tasha wasn't willing to wait for that outcome.

Who was chasing her mother? Who were the men in the alley? So far she hadn't seen any sign of them since coming to Forever, but would that last? And were they the only ones her mother was running from?

The men were right. But that didn't change the fact that she had to find her mother first. Once she did, she'd make her mother tell her the complete truth.

From what she'd read about the chupacabra, the creature didn't go around biting people and changing them. The most horrifying fact about them was that they drained the blood from their victims like canine vampires. Yet even that wasn't a confirmed fact. Misinformation and misunderstanding swirled around the chupacabra. Most wouldn't even admit they existed. Yet she knew the truth. She'd seen her mother transform into one of them.

She didn't hear the phone call over the roar of the vehicle, but she felt the vibration against her hip. Slowing down, she steered over to the side of the road then pulled the phone out of her pocket.

The caller ID said it was a private name. She answered, her hand shaking. "Mom? Is that you?"

She waited, her breath held. If her mother had a phone and was calling, then that meant she was back in human form. Was she camped nearby? "Mom?" Soon enough, however, she realized that the call had already ended. She stared at the phone, willing her mother— providing the call had truly been from her mother—to call back. Her heart sank as the phone remained silent.

Then the tweet announcing a text came. Her heart picked up speed.

Go home.
It's her.

Tasha gripped the phone tightly. It had to be her mother. She texted back as fast as she could.

Where are you?

It's too dangerous for you here. Go home.

Her thumbs flew over the keys. *Tell me where you are. I can help you.*

You weren't supposed to come. Not yet. Not until…go home. Now. Please.

Who are those men? Who's after you?

Men who want to hurt me.

Because of what you are?

Yes.

Then don't change again.

Go home.

Come home with me. I'll keep you safe.

You can't. Please. Go home. I never should have involved you.

But you did, so let me help.

No. Go home. I love you.

Tell me where you are. We'll find a way.

She waited and waited some more, but no answer came. "No, Mom. Don't stop." Yet the phone remained mute.

She sat down on the ATV, the strength in her legs suddenly gone. Glancing around, she wondered, not for the first time, if she was making a mistake. But leaving her mother behind was something she couldn't do.

If only I had someone to help me.

Her thoughts turned to the men at the ranch. If anyone could find her mother, she bet they could. Did she dare ask them? Would they believe her? And if they found out about her mother, could she trust them to keep her secret?

* * * *

Wick wasn't about to give up. If luck was with him, he'd hear the ATV and pick up her trail. Sitting back and doing nothing wasn't his way.

Wick's front paws hit the ground minutes before his brothers had finished shifting. He pounded after Tasha, fearing the way she'd barreled out of there. The girl could drive an ATV, but that didn't mean she knew how to control it going at breakneck speed. They could've hopped into the pickup and chased after her, and maybe even caught up with her, but then she would've known they were on her tail. Chasing her as wolves would be easier and faster as they zipped over the countryside, leaving the man-made trails behind. Hopefully, he'd cut across the right path and find her.

His brothers had to be thinking the same thing. Something wasn't right, and they were bound and determined to figure what out what that something was. As they'd questioned her, he'd sensed her tenseness and had smelled the anxiety flowing off her. She was afraid of something, yet he didn't think she was afraid for herself. But then, if not for herself, then who? A man? His gut twisted thinking about the possibility. But if it wasn't a man, then who?

Paul raced past him, followed on his heels by Shane. Wick wouldn't let them get ahead of him. He concentrated on putting his paws in the right place and letting his wolf run free. His mate, their mate, needed them, and nothing and no one would get in their way to help her.

* * * *

By the time Tasha had made it home, she'd been exhausted. She'd driven farther than she ever had, yet had come up empty once again. The house had been dark, the men obviously gone somewhere, by the time she'd stumbled into her camper and fallen into her bed. She'd been too exhausted to care that she hadn't gotten to see them again.

Yet that was probably a good thing. No doubt, they would have started questioning her more.

But now, fresh from a morning shower, she was eager to see them. She'd nix the questions fast enough. Besides, she had the feeling that they'd gotten the hint to stop prying from her abrupt departure yesterday.

She yearned to see them. Not that she'd ever let them know. A woman had to have some pride. Keeping them guessing would be a good thing. After all, she felt a little ridiculous, having run off the way she had. Why compound that feeling by drooling over them?

She stepped out of the camper and looked around. She could hear them, but she couldn't see them. From the distance, between sounds, she could tell they weren't together in one spot.

"Take it easy. No one's going to hurt you."

At first, she thought Shane must've been talking to her. The sound of his voice soothed her. Then, once she'd figured out that he wasn't talking to her, she was disappointed. His voice was like velvet and filled with a warm richness that consoled her, comforted her, and make her feel safe even as it turned her on. Was he talking to another woman? She fisted her hands at the thought.

She strode toward the sound, all the while preparing herself to find him with someone else. Jealousy hit her even harder, and she tried to force it away. If he was with a woman, what could she do? Pretend a casualness she didn't feel? Or turn around and stalk off? It wasn't as though she could accuse him of anything. After all, what right did she have getting jealous? She didn't even know the man. Yet there it was, the green-eyed monster alive and well, churning in her stomach.

She rounded the corner and entered the barn. Forgetting her reasoning, she was ready with heated words on the tip of her tongue, ready to chastise him for being with someone else. Then she saw the object of his soothing vocal caresses.

Shane's green eyes met hers. "Hey, darlin', how are you doing this morning?"

Not for the first time since meeting him, she felt ridiculous. Ridiculous and horny as hell. She came to a stop, all too aware that she'd been jealous of a horse.

He frowned when she didn't answer. "Are you all right?"

Irritation for getting jealous transferred to him. She fisted her hands, ready to blast him.

Why didn't you follow me? Why didn't you chase after me and bring me back? Don't you give a damn?

Thankfully, she kept the questions to herself. She had no right, much less a reason, to expect Shane or the other men to care. Why she was upset that they didn't care was beyond her. "I'm fine. I just—"

"You just what?"

Strangely, she had a feeling that he knew exactly what she'd almost said. That she'd wanted to tell him to touch her like that, to talk sweetly to her. She broke her gaze from his. "Nothing." She jerked her chin toward the horse. "And who's this?"

Pride brightened his expression. "This is my favorite female in the whole world. This is Shania Twain."

She laughed. "Shania Twain? Like the country singer?"

He shrugged, the corners of his mouth lifting. "What can I say? I had a crush on Shania. For a while, I named all the horses after my favorite country singers. We used to own Garth, Reba, and three little fillies named after The Dixie Chicks."

"Seriously?"

He placed a palm over his heart. "I cannot tell a lie. Yeah. I know it was silly, but what the hell? It was fun."

"Can I pet her?" She'd never been much of a country girl. Had, in fact, never done much outside the city.

"'Course you can. Don't worry. She's gentle."

At that moment, Tasha couldn't have told anyone who she was more intrigued with, the horse or the man. Strangely, right then, it didn't matter. She came toward the horse and slowly lifted her hand. Taking a moment to make sure the animal was all right with her movements, she gently stroked its neck. "She's so soft."

"Most beautiful females are."

His hand took hers, startling her. Again, their gazes met and locked. The strange feeling she'd felt before revved up even more, speeding faster and wilder. She didn't understand it, but she loved it all the same. It was like a drug she was already hooked on.

"Try here." He moved her hand to the horse's muzzle.

Only the sweet softness of the horse could've broken the spell his eyes held on her. "Oooh," she murmured. "I've never felt anything so soft."

"It's something, isn't it?"

A yearning in his tone had her looking up once again, searching his face. She wanted to reach out and stroke his cheek as she'd done the horses'. "Shania is a good name for her. She has the same hair color. But can she sing?"

His chuckle warmed her. "That's a good one."

"How many horses do you have?"

"Do you really want to know? Or are there better questions you should be asking?"

She jerked her hand away from the horse, suddenly wary. "I don't know what you mean."

He shrugged then ran his hand along the horse's rump. "Better yet, there are questions I'd rather be asking."

She knew better than to ask, yet she did anyway. "Like what?"

"Questions that would help me keep you safe. Questions that would help me understand you better."

She hadn't expected him to say he actually cared. Still, she had to ask, "Because you care?"

His nod was barely perceptible, yet it was as forceful as a shout. "Yeah. Because I care."

Did he? Did all of them care? But how? Emotions were coming too fast to trust them. She struggled to drag in a breath even as her heart sang with the possibilities. Did she care for them? Again, it was ridiculous to think so, but there it was.

She closed her eyes and forced her thoughts away. Now was not the time to fall in love. Not with one man, let alone three.

"Tasha? What's going on?"

She let out the breath she hadn't realized she was holding. As soon as her gaze met his, she jerked it away. "Nothing."

Yet what would happen if she told him? She'd thought about it all night long, and now here it was again. What if the men could help? What if she told them and they believed her? Yet uncertainty held her back.

"Tell me, Tasha. Let me help you."

As if his words weren't enough to encourage her, he took her by the arms and forced her to stare at him again. Oh, how she wanted to tell him.

"Tell me." As though he gave it more consideration, he added, "Either start talking, or I won't be responsible for what I do next."

Her gaze dropped to his mouth. It was firm, yet soft. Another soft area she wanted to explore. "What are you going to do?"

He closed his eyes. His struggle to maintain control evident in the clenching of his jaw. When he opened them again, amber flecks dotted the green. "This."

The kiss caught her off-guard. It was firm, yet gentle. Heated and needy as his tongue flicked over the crease of her mouth. She moaned and leaned against him, encouraging him to do more. Yet if he only kissed her, she would be satisfied.

For now.

But his kiss continued as his hands discovered her body. He

cupped her breast, his thumb massaging her hardening nipple. He fondled her butt cheek, his fingers digging into her ass. She moaned again and wrapped her arms around his neck.

Passion welled inside her. Where there had been a spark before, flames now burn brightly. The hunger for him that had started the moment she'd seen him, doubled, then tripled, then grew ten times as great. She craved him, yearned for him. If he didn't touch her in every way, in every place, she'd go insane.

He picked her up until she could wrap her legs around his waist. His hard cock pressed against her crotch, and she worked her hips, wishing their clothes would disappear. A groan rumbled through his chest, making her think of an animal. If he wanted to take her like an animal, she wouldn't resist. Hell, she'd urged him on.

His hands were everywhere now, slipping underneath her clothes to find hidden places she hadn't shown to many men. Her nipples ached for his mouth, and as though he understood, he pulled her shirt apart and put his mouth to the hard bud. She arched her back and ground her crotch against him even harder.

His words were muffled by her breast, but she understood. He wanted her as much as she wanted him. "Put me down."

He resisted at first then set her on her feet. "Don't leave." It was both a command and a plea.

"No." She took a step back then began undoing the buttons of her shirt. She hadn't planned to have sex with him, with any of them, but right then it was the most important thing in the world for her to do.

He tugged his shirt over his head and tossed it aside then went to work on his belt buckle. "Are you sure, darlin'?" Before she could say anything, he shook his head. "No. Forget I asked."

She had just tugged her shirt out of her jeans when her phone vibrated in her pocket. Indecision wafted over her. She didn't want to stop what was about to happen, but what if it was her mother calling? "I'm sorry," she said, the pain evident in her tone.

As she stepped back, he came toward her. "No. Don't answer it.

No call could be that important."

"I'm sorry." She whirled around, pulling the phone from her pocket and striding toward the barn entrance. By the time she was out in the sunlight, by the time she'd buttoned her shirt, and by the time she realized he hadn't followed her, she knew it wasn't her mother calling.

Damn it.

She turned to go back inside the barn when it hit her. Maybe it was for the best. Maybe the spam caller had saved her in the nick of time.

What she'd been ready to do could've changed her entire life. She had a job to do, a purpose for being where she was, and that didn't include getting involved with a handsome man. Instead of going back inside the barn, she whirled around and strode toward the sounds coming from behind the house.

She found Wick chopping wood. His shirt was off and lying over a pile of wood. His tanned bronze skin glistened under the sun, droplets of sweat sparkling against his body. She sucked in a quick breath, momentarily mesmerized by the country Adonis. His body was toned without an ounce of body fat. His lean waist and his ripped abdomen tensed as he lifted the axe above his head then brought it down on the piece of wood, splintering it in half. Muscles rippled in his arms as he brought the axe up again and again. She might've stood there, unnoticed, for an undetermined length of time if he hadn't stopped to wipe his brow and turned to see her.

"Hey, I didn't see you there. Did you need something?"

Yeah. You.

Thankfully, once again, she didn't say the words out loud. Instead, she shook her head and tried to think straight. "No. Nothing. I was just kind of taking a walk." She hoped she didn't sound as lame as she thought she did.

He leaned the axe against the stump. His legs ate up the distance between them as he strode toward her. The closer he got, the more forceful the sensation inside her grew. What was it that stirred her emotions so much? It was more than simple attraction, but she couldn't put a name to it.

Yet maybe that's the way real love works.

Love?

Oh hell. Stop thinking like a teenage girl.

Yet if any man inspired romance, it was Wick. His dark eyes sparkled, a sexy gleam lighting them even as she saw bits of amber burst to life. Her breath came in quick pants, and for a moment, she felt woozy. "I don't mean to interrupt—"

Before she could finish the sentence, he grabbed a hold of her and drew her into his arms. Her breath left her in a whoosh of air.

"I can't put this off any longer." His tone was gruff, husky, his need all too apparent.

He kissed her then, roughly, without a hint of softness. As different as it was to Shane's kiss, she, nonetheless, loved it. She made a whimpering sound as she clung to his shoulders, his sweat wetting her fingers. He bent her backward with the force of his kiss, and her hair fell away from her shoulders. Unable to resist, she kissed him back.

Her hands slipped to his broad chest and felt his warmth under her palms. She swore she could feel his heart beating rapidly, matching her own fast heartbeat.

She should stop him, but she was still purring from the attention Shane had given her. The need she'd experienced with Shane burned brightly again, this time growing even hotter.

Wick broke the kiss and lifted her into his arms, much as Shane had done. Taking her with him, he set her down on top of the nearby woodpile then tore at her blouse, undoing the buttons as fast as he could. Once he had her shirt parted, his mouth found her breast and latched onto her nipple. She leaned backward, her hands pressed against the hard wood, her chest thrust toward him.

Fuck me, please. Fuck me.

His hands gripped her jeans and, with one hard yank, brought them to her knees. Her panties were gone in the next instant. Taking hold of her ass cheeks, he slid his tongue down and over the rise of her stomach. With one quick look, he knelt between her legs and shoved them wide.

Oh, yeah, she thought as a moan rolled out of her.

Putting her legs over his shoulders, he dove in and put his mouth to her pussy. She let out a small yelp and threw her head back. He ate at her, devouring her with his teeth, nibbling at her aching clit. His tongue swirled around, over, then dipped inside, drinking all her juices. He sucked, he bit, he swiped his tongue over her throbbing clit again and again.

The climax hit her hard and fast, threatening to make her lose all sense of equilibrium. Her body shuddered as her release stormed through her. Yet he didn't stop.

She cried out in the pain of ecstasy as yet another climax grew in the wake of the first one. Could she withstand the pain? Would her release come before she broke apart? When it came, it came hard and fast, tearing her apart and rending another cry from her.

When at last he stood, he wiped her juices from his face. "Now it's my turn, baby."

Her chest heaved with her labored breaths as she stared at him, trying to comprehend what had happened. *How* it had happened. She wanted him, especially when he undid his belt buckle and pulled the flap of his jeans apart. His huge cock stuck out and pointed straight at her.

"Fuck that."

Although she recognized Paul's voice, she still had a difficult time believing he was there. Where had he come from?

"We weren't going to do this. Not yet." Paul shoved Wick aside then planted his feet apart as though ready to fight.

Wick's face, contorted into a snarl, was more animal than human. "I don't give a crap what we said."

Paul's gaze scanned her body, and she could see from the gleam in his eye that he wanted her as much as she wanted him. Still, she could also see that he struggled, unwilling to give into the passion that was flamed in his eyes.

She stood up, pulling her jeans up and tugging her shirt together. She should've been embarrassed as any self-respecting woman would be, but she wasn't. Everything she'd—no, they'd—done had felt right. So very right.

Paul couldn't hide his need. Not when the bulge in his jeans was plain enough to see. Still, he didn't move. Did he have that much control? She didn't think he did. She knew she didn't. "Kiss me."

"Back off, Paul," warned Wick.

Paul shook his head again. "We said we weren't going to do this. But I'll be damned if I'm the only one that doesn't get a taste of you."

With a frustrated groan, he clutched her by the back of her head, holding a hunk of her hair to keep her still. Then, just as she parted her lips in welcome, he kissed her. His kiss, too, was different than Wick's, different than Shane's. Yet it was just as sexy, just as needy. His tongue swept into her mouth to taste all of her flavors. She grabbed hold of his arms, doing her best to hold him to her.

The kiss deepened as a growl rumbled through his chest. The sound was animalistic, as though he'd suddenly transformed into a cave man, primal and demanding. She had no more choice with him than she'd had with his brothers. She kissed him back, fervently, ready to submit to his wishes.

She almost broke apart when he ended the kiss. "Why?" she whispered, certain she'd spoken so softly that he couldn't have heard her. Her knees weakened as she sought to sit down on the logs. Then she'd open her legs for him, too. But he wouldn't let her. Instead, he made certain she was steady on her feet then turned her loose.

"Don't you want me?" she asked, this time in a voice that he'd be sure to hear.

"Are you kidding me? Of course I do. You know I do."

"Then why'd you stop?" She had no shame. She wanted them. Nothing else, no one else would ever satisfy her.

"Get inside, everyone," he demanded, his voice husky with his craving. "There are things that have to be said first." He reached out to take her arm then, suddenly, turned it loose.

Was he afraid to touch her and be tempted yet again?

Before she could ask, Wick held out his hand, and she gladly took it. He led her toward the house as Paul called out to Shane, who strode out of the barn and followed them inside.

Paul waved her to the couch, asking her sit in the middle. Fear slipped into her, melting in with the passion. She did as he asked even as she thought about running toward the camper. Yet she was so drawn to them that she couldn't force herself to move.

He took a seat on the coffee table in front of her while Wick and Shane sat on either side of her. "We don't have to tell you that we want you. We proved as much today." He glanced toward Shane. "I'm betting all of us?"

"Yeah. In the barn," answered Shane.

A lift of Paul's eyebrows was his only response to finding out that Shane and she had had their own time. Perhaps they hadn't gone as far as she and Wick had, but it had still been hot and…meaningful. At least, to her. But were the encounters as meaningful to them?

"Before we get any farther into the sexual part of our relationship"—one of Paul's eyebrows arched even higher—"we have to know what's going on."

She squirmed in her seat, knowing she had little recourse except to answer. "I'm not sure I should tell you."

"Why not, darlin'?" asked Shane. "You can trust us."

"How do I know that?"

Now it was Shane who arched an eyebrow. "You just know."

Yes, I do.

"Tell us," urged Wick.

She couldn't figure out a better way to explain why she kept her secret, so she just spit it out. "Because I don't think you'd believe me. Hell, I wouldn't believe me, either, if I were you."

"Baby, you'd be surprised at what we'd believe. Just tell us."

She wanted to believe Wick, wanted to tell them, yet she held back. Whatever was happening between them, she didn't want to ruin it with a fantastic tale. Even a fantastic tale that was true. Nothing would ruin their relationship faster than them thinking she was crazy. Still, the urge to tell them was hard to ignore. "What if I tell you and you don't believe me?"

"You're never going to know until you tell us." Paul leaned even closer. "Tell us."

What other choice did she have? If she left now, she'd have to take her camper and leave for good. There was no way she'd be able to resist them, especially now that they'd touched and kissed. Being so close to them would only end up bringing them together once again. As much as she might try, she couldn't keep secrets and be intimate. Not if she wanted even a small chance at getting to know them better.

"I'm here to find my mother."

Judging by their expressions, her response was the last thing they'd expected her to say.

* * * *

"Well, hell, that's the last thing I expected to hear," proclaimed Shane.

She shot them a "well, you asked for it" look. "But that's why I'm here. I'm looking for my mother."

"You're looking for your mother out in the middle of nowhere Texas? What's she doing out here?" Paul looked to his brothers for an answer, but they had none.

"This isn't going to be easy to explain."

"Give it a shot," urged Wick. "Whatever it is, we'll listen with an open mind."

She dragged in a breath. "Okay. Here goes. Just promise me you'll listen to all of it before you pass judgment." She glared at them in warning. "Plus, you have to promise you won't laugh at me."

"We swear," said Wick.

"A short while ago, my mother told me that she had been attacked by a wild animal." She studied their reactions and was surprised to see that they weren't all that surprised. But why? How many people got attacked by wild animals? More than she would've imagined?

"Go on, sugar." Paul's voice was soft, encouraging.

"Okay. Well, when she was attacked by this animal, she said it changed her." She waited for them to respond, to ask questions, to do something. Instead, they simply sat where they were and waited. "Should I go on?" At their nods, she did.

"Anyway—and this is the part that's going to sound really crazy—she said it changed her into the same kind of animal." Again, no response. It was as though they'd heard the story before.

"What kind of animal?" asked Wick.

She was relieved that one of them had finally said something. "The animal that bit her, the animal she can change into now is a"— she drew in another steadying breath—"chupacabra."

At least now they showed a reaction. And, as she'd guessed from the beginning, their reactions were ones of disbelief.

"Those things don't exist."

She twisted to confront the skeptical Shane. "That's what everyone thinks. But I'm here to tell you that they do."

"Because your mother says she was bitten and changed by one? Is that what you're telling us?"

So now Paul doubted her? After assuring her they'd listen with an open mind? Still, how could she blame him? Her story was an incredible one. "That's what I'm telling you."

Wick chuckled. "Baby, I've seen a lot of weird things in this world, but I've never seen one of those. I've never even met anyone who has. And trust me, if they existed, we'd know."

"Then I guess you don't know everything, do you?" She crossed her arms, ready to meet their challenge.

"Tell us the rest," urged Paul. "Because there's got to be more to the story than that."

She rankled at his use of the word "story" but bit back a retort.

"How do you know your mother is telling you the truth?" Shane started to touch her then withdrew his hand at her hard look.

Irritation flared. "Why should I think my mother's lying? And why should you?"

Shane leaned back as though he thought she might strike him, as though her words could physically harm him. "Hang on. I'm not calling your mother a liar. I'm just trying to understand."

"Yeah," interjected Paul. "All we're doing is asking for some evidence."

"And you've seen one?" asked Wick.

"Have you?" challenged Paul.

"Yes, I have."

"And what did it look like?"

"It looked kind of like a dog only more skeletal and without fur. It has these ridges or spine things running down its back." She hated how she'd sounded. "Not it. My mother. I think I saw my mother's eyes turn red, too." She did her best to recall all the details, but her mother had been hidden in the alley's shadows.

"Are you sure what you saw wasn't a dog? Or maybe a coyote?"

She wanted to hurl curses at Wick yet there was a softening, a questioning on his face that gave her hope that he was finally beginning to believe her. "I know what I saw. It—my mother—wasn't a dog or a coyote." She narrowed her eyes. "Or even a wolf." She wasn't sure why she'd added the last part.

"And your mother has been changed into one of them?" Paul frowned, yet she could see his determination weaken as he started to believe her.

"Yes. Damn it. I saw her change. I saw her transform from a woman into that creature."

Chapter Four

"Okay," said Paul. "Let's assume what you're telling us is the truth."

If Tasha gritted her teeth any harder, she'd break one. "It *is* the truth. Either you believe me or you don't."

"We're not saying we don't," added Wick. "It's just that we've never seen one. Especially around Forever." He glanced at Paul. "Still, we've heard stories…"

"Which is why I doubt"—Paul lifted his hands defensively—"that it's real. If anyone would've seen one, especially around these parts, it's us. Some myths really are only myths."

"Yeah, but stranger things have happened." Shane seemed preoccupied with his own thoughts as though trying to solve a problem. A frown worried his brow. "She's right. We don't know everything, and I doubt we've seen everything."

"We have when it comes to Forever," asserted Paul.

"My mother was bitten and changed overseas, not here."

"Not in Forever, huh?" Shane shot a look at the others. "That makes a difference, right? We don't know what might exist in other countries."

"I don't get it. You act like you three are experts on the shape-shifters. Are you? Because if you're not, then you can't say for a fact that chupacabras don't exist. I know for a fact that they do. I saw my mother change."

"Again, she has a point," added Shane. "We've seen a lot, but we haven't seen everything. Not by a long shot, I'll bet. Besides, if she says she saw her mother change, then I believe her. What would be the point of her making this shit up?"

"True enough." Paul crossed his arms, a look of consideration coming to his face. "So you're out hunting for your mother every night. But how do you know she's here? And how do you think you're going to catch a chupacabra? To catch her? What are you planning on doing? Running over her with the ATV? Shooting her in the ass then taking her back to the camper and tucking into your bed? Or do you think you can just whistle and expect her to come to you?"

"Damn it, Paul, don't be an asshole," warned Wick.

She was on her feet, clenching her hands. "My mother is a notable scientist. She was doing research when she was bitten. When I met with her and she told me what had happened, she gave me a tracking device and told me to recover her body if she was killed."

"Why didn't she stay with you in the first place?" asked Paul. "Why doesn't she come to you now that you're here?"

"I don't know. Maybe she's trying to keep me safe. She told me she was going to somewhere around Forever. I don't know everything that's going on, but I know enough to believe what my mother said. There are people after her. I saw them. I don't know if they want her technology, or if they want her because of what she now is. All I know is that I have to find her before they do. Before it really is her dead body I find. Look, if you don't want to help me, then just say so."

"Take it easy, darlin'," cooed Shane. "This is a lot to take in."

She'd had it with them. Her hopes of them helping her were gone.

"Darlin', give us some time to let this sink in," asked Shane. "To come up with a plan."

She studied Shane. Of the three of them, he seemed ready to believe her.

"Yeah, sugar," added Paul.

She didn't need them. After all, she'd started on the mission by herself, and she'd end it by herself. "You know what? Fuck you. I don't need your help, and I don't want it."

"Don't go being like that, sugar." Paul stood, ready to take her into her arms. "You know we'll help you, but we don't want to jump into this thing half-cocked. Do you know anything about the people who are after her?"

She backed away, unwilling to be touched. "No. But it has to be for one reason or the other. Either they're after some kind of new technology she's devised, or they want her for what she's become."

"It wouldn't be the first time people have tried to capture a"—Wick stalled, suddenly watching his words—"a special kind of animal."

She whirled around and headed for the door. They came after her, as she knew they would, but she turned to confront them. "Back the hell off. I'll get my camper and be off your land as soon as I can."

"Baby, come on. Let's talk."

"Don't call me baby." She looked back once more then slammed the door in the faces. To make matters worse, she had to fight the tears stinging her eyes as she hurried across the yard toward her camper.

* * * *

As he had done so often that day, Shane looked out the window and checked once again. "Well, at least she hasn't moved yet." To his relief, the camper was still in the same place.

"Hopefully, she changed her mind. Let's let her cool off a bit before we approach her again." Paul flipped open the barrel of the gun, checked to see that it was empty, then flipped it shut. As a rule, werewolves didn't like guns and usually didn't own them, but Paul was the exception. Not that Shane understood it, but his brother like to go target shooting.

They hadn't spoken much since Tasha had left. Shane wasn't happy about the silence between them, but he knew it wouldn't last long. Sooner or later, they'd have to talk about what she'd told them.

He guessed now was as good a time as any.

"So? What do you think about what she told us?" asked Shane.

"Her mother is a chupacabra." Wick chuckled as he plopped the *Horseman* magazine he'd been reading back on the coffee table. "I don't know about you two, but that's was one hell of a story. Strangest thing I've ever heard."

"Does that mean you don't believe her?" Shane intended to ease into the truth. Until now, he'd never mentioned what he'd seen. Until now, until after Tasha had described her mother, he'd believed something entirely different.

"I'm not saying that. But, damn it, we've lived here all of our lives, and I've never seen anything like what she's talking about. According to what I've found online, a chupacabra is a doglike creature that has spines jutting out along his back. The thing has red eyes and has no fur. That's exactly how Tasha described it. Even stranger, it's supposed to suck the blood from all of its prey. Kind of like a vampire dog."

At least Paul had done a little research. Which, to Shane's thinking, meant he, too, had accepted Tasha's story. "Just because we haven't seen one, doesn't mean it doesn't exist."

"Yeah, it kind of does." Wick put his boots on top of the coffee table. He let out a breath. "Or at least, it used to."

"A lot of people would say that about werewolves. They've never seen one, so they don't believe they exist. We know better than anyone that there are a lot of things in this world that remained hidden. That doesn't mean they aren't real."

Both his brothers stopped what they were doing and coolly regarded him. But he'd gone too far to turn back now.

Paul's eyes narrowed. "We believe her. But why do I get the feeling you're trying to tell us something more?"

"Yeah, Paul's dead-on. You're hiding something. Just spit it out."

Shane stuck his hands in his pockets and wished he'd told his brothers a long time ago. But after that night when he'd almost run headlong into the animal, he'd talked himself into believing it had been a coyote. A mean-looking one, but he'd barely gotten a look at the animal before it had vanished into the bushes. Plus, he'd drunk a shitload of tequila before he'd shifted and gone for the run. Then, as time passed, he'd simply forgotten about it. Until now.

He ground his teeth, reconsidered, then blurted out the truth. "I've think I've seen one." *Red eyes. No fur.* "Yeah. I've seen a chupacabra."

"That's bullshit," challenged Paul. "Or is that your way of cozying up to Tasha?"

"Sorry, man, but I'm telling you the truth."

"When did you see it?" asked Wick. "Are you telling us you've seen her mother?"

He shook his head, almost wishing he could've said yes. "No. It's been a couple years, and at the time I wasn't sure what I'd seen. But since we've been talking about chupacabras, I realize now that what I saw was one of them."

"This happened two years ago and you're just now telling us? That doesn't make any sense."

He could tell Paul was ticked off. That, perhaps, he was even hurt that Shane had kept a secret. "I was drunk and out running when I ran into the damn thing. It was a small animal, but strong as hell. Damn thing knocked me off my paws. Plus, it was dark, and the thing moved super-fast. I was still trying to figure out what had happened by the time it had already gone. We're fast, but that animal was a hell of a lot faster than a werewolf. Later, I figured it had to have been a strange-looking coyote."

Wick leaned back and ran a hand through his hair. "And now you think it was one of these things?" Wick stood and paced to the other side of the room. "This is fucked up, man. Damn it. Why didn't you tell us earlier?"

"You screwed up. Why didn't you say something back then?" asked Paul. "And why didn't you say something in front of Tasha?"

Why hadn't he? Yet Shane didn't have an answer. "I don't know. Like I said before, I chalked it up to my being drunk. At least, until now."

The sound of horse's neigh—too close to be coming from the barn—interrupted their conversation. Along with his brothers, Shane went to the window and looked out. "Shit. Is she serious?"

Wick chuckled. "I'd say she's as serious as a heart attack."

Tasha had led one of the horses out of the barn. "Why is she taking one of our horses? Why not take her ATV?" He jerked back from the window as she turned to look at the house.

"Maybe she thinks she'll have better luck if she doesn't have the sound of an engine scaring her mother off. Or maybe she's trying to sneak out and thinks we'll hear the motor turning over."

Shane figured Paul was right. But whatever her reason, she was heading out on her own. No doubt, she was going after her mother.

He stepped away from the window and began taking off his clothes, getting ready to shift. As the transformation swept over him, the pain coming as it always did as his bones broke and reformed, he asked his brothers, "Are we following her or not?"

His question, however, was not needed. They'd already begun changing. More questions filtered through his half-wolf, half-human mind.

Can we keep up with her? And if they could, and she found her mother, what then?

* * * *

Tasha wasn't sure that the men would see her taking a horse as "borrowing" it, but she'd had no other choice. If they heard her leave on the ATV, she was certain they would come after her. After saddling the horse—thank goodness for summer camp and riding lessons—then it leading out of the barn, she'd swung herself into the saddle, then looked to the house. If she was lucky, they wouldn't come out to the barn. And even if they did, she could give the horse a good heel and get away before they could stop her. Even if they tried to follow her, she'd have a head start on them. They wouldn't be able to track her in the dark and off the well-traveled paths. At least, she hoped they wouldn't.

Or did she? Even now, as she leaned over the horse and urged it forward into the darkness, she wished she had the men beside her. If anyone could help her find her mother, it was them.

Locating her mother was proving harder than she'd ever thought it would be. The tracking device was useful, but every time she thought she'd found her mother, her mother would take off. The tracking blimp would move quickly across the screen.

Each time she went out, hoping she'd find her mother alive and well, she always ended up disappointed. At this point, she had to wonder if she should simply give up. Or wait until the awful day when she had to retrieve her mother's dead body. Yet she couldn't give up. As estranged as she and her mother were, she still cared for her. She still longed for a relationship.

If only I didn't care.

"Where are you, Mother?" She glanced at the tracker, showing her mother in the nearby vicinity, then looked around her. How close was she? How accurate was the device? Yet, even without the tracker, she could feel in her bones that her mother was close by.

Was her mother hiding from her? Or did her mother not know her while she was in her animal body? Did the animal she became retain a sense of humanity? Even if she found her mother, would she have to use the gun to bring her to bay? Or would her attempts to locate her mother once again turn out to be futile?

She'd been riding for at least an hour when, suddenly, the horse reared up on its hind legs and kicked its front legs out, whinnying a terrified sound. A dark form streaked across the path in front of her. Tasha held on to the saddle horn, gripping it as tightly as possible to stay on top of the animal. The horse reared up again a second time, but this time Tasha was prepared.

"Whoa. Whoa there."

The horse continued to dance, its ears flicking back and forth, trying to pick up the sound of an attacker. Tasha leaned over and patted the animal's neck as she scanned the area. The moon was only half full, giving partial light.

"Easy, boy. Whatever it was is gone now." *Damn it. What if it was my mother?*

Although she hadn't gotten a good glimpse of what had dashed out in front of them, she sensed it was her mother. She was so close, yet so far.

She'd just gotten the horse to settle down when the animal reared yet again. Once more, the dark form raced across their path. The frightened horse, its nerves already jangled, rose up on his back legs for a third time. Tasha lost her grip. She let out a cry as she tumbled backward off the horse.

She hit the ground hard, the air knocked from her. For a moment, she lay there looking up at the night sky and wondering what had happened. The horse pranced nearby, jerking its head up and down several times as it snorted its fear. Then, without warning, the horse spun around and dashed down the path.

Tasha hurried to get on her feet and called out to the animal, but it was too late. The horse was long gone.

Shit. What the hell am I going to do now?

Gone was her ride. And, perhaps even worse, gone was her gun. She was alone and defenseless. Having hoped the horse could help her find their way back to the ranch house, she realized she had no sense of which direction to go.

"Damn it all to hell. I shouldn't ever have taken that horse. At least the ATV wouldn't have run off and left me."

A low growl had her turning slowly around. Fear swept its way through her.

The animal stood at the edge of the path, half hidden by the brush.

Red eyes glared at her. A long muzzle sported sharp fangs. As it stepped out onto the path, she had no doubt about what it was.

A chupacabra.

But was this her mother?

The beast crept slowly toward her, its head lowered as it crouched, ready to spring at her. The long furless tail dipped between its legs.

"Mom? Is that you?" she whispered. If it were her mother, would her mother still know her? And if it weren't her mother, how would she defend herself?

Again, she wished that the men had come with her. If only her temper hadn't gotten the best of her, maybe she could've convinced them that her story was real. But the time for that had passed.

She wasn't sure what to do. Should she crouch lower to appear less threatening? Or should she make herself taller to appear more imposing?

Just as she was about to crouch and pray she was doing the right thing, the chupacabra snarled, its glowing red gaze shifting to a position over her shoulder. Tasha glanced behind her to find two men with rifles standing at the edge of the brushes. The moon was behind them, shadowing their faces.

Hoping she was right, hoping the chupacabra was indeed her mother, she put her body directly between the men and the animal. "Leave her alone," she demanded.

"Kill her, too." The man's voice was gravelly and devoid of any emotion.

The chill of real fear stiffened her. Her mind screamed to get out of the way. She was risking her life for an animal that might not even be her mother. Yet she stayed where she was.

The darkness obscured their movements, but she sensed that they'd lifted the rifles to their shoulders, ready to fire. The animal behind her growled, but she didn't turn. If the animal attacked her while her back was turned, then so be it. But she had to have faith that the beast was, in fact, her mother.

"Leave her alone. Leave us alone." Yet she had no power, no real means to keep them from hurting them.

The men's heads tilted to the side as though they were getting ready to aim their weapons. She closed her eyes, ready to accept her fate.

"Run, Mother. Run," she whispered. She closed her eyes, unwilling to know the exact moment they fired. She got ready to feel the pain of the bullets slashing through her body.

Growls, more than any one animal could make, ripped into her. She jolted as though the growls had physically torn her apart. Were there other chupacabras? Was there a pack of them?

Yet, did it matter now? There was nothing she could do to save herself. Hopefully, the pack would protect her mother. She drew in what could possibly be her last breath and, once more, prepared to be attacked by animals or shot.

When the shot didn't come, when the growls turned to snarls that weren't accompanied by razor-sharp claws and teeth tearing into her flesh, she dared to open her eyes. The two men with rifles were gone. A flash of fur disappeared into the night.

"Mom?" She whirled around, ready to find out once and for all if the animal was her mother. But the chupacabra was gone.

No. Please. Not again.

Yet she'd told her mother to run, and her mother had done exactly that. "Damn."

Sensing the presence of someone watching her, Tasha stiffened again and forced herself to turn back. "Oh shit."

Three wolves, one black, one brown, and one with lighter fur, stood in a line in the same place where the men with rifles had stood. They were enormous animals, their size at least triple that of a normal wolf. Powerful muscles rippled under their fur. Instead of the red eyes of the chupacabra, glowing amber locked onto her.

Are you fucking kidding me? First men with rifles, then a chupacabra pack, and now wolves? When am I going to catch a break?

A giggle, not born of mirth, but of astonishment escaped her.

She swallowed hard, finding it difficult to breathe. Once again, she found herself in a vulnerable position. Should they attack her, she'd have no way to defend against them. Keeping them in view, she looked around, searching for anything she could use as a weapon. Grabbing a large rock, she lifted it above her head and tried to appear as threatening as possible.

But the wolves didn't budge. Their eyes never blinked. Slowly, silently, they padded toward her.

Needing to do something, anything, she stuck out her hand, palm out, and demanded in the most commanding voice she could, "Stay back. Go away!"

The wolves stopped. Strangely, she would've bet money that they'd understood what she'd said. Had, she believed, responded to her demand more than to the tone of her voice.

Do they understand me?

She lowered the rock for a moment then quickly lifted it again. "Go away! I don't want to hurt you, but I will. I'm not an easy prey." She'd almost forgotten about the rock she held but raised it even higher. "Get away! Shoo!"

The golden-furred one tilted its head to the side. If she hadn't known better, she would've sworn it was smiling. Or was it laughing at her?

"Get! Shoo!" She dared to step forward, doing her best to scare them away. "Get out of here, damn it!"

The black wolf, slightly larger than the other two, lowered its head and growled. Yet the growl wasn't meant for her, as it looked to first one then the other wolf. The other two wolves dipped their heads as though nodding their agreement.

She didn't dare speak again. If they were going to leave, they'd do it now. Or was the leader telling them to get ready to attack?

Suddenly, the leader wagged its tail. She blinked, unwilling to trust its change in demeanor. Then, with a quick flick of its tail, the large black wolf whirled around and dashed into the bushes. The other two wolves followed him.

Relief flooded her. Her legs lost the ability to keep her standing, and she slumped to the ground.

* * * *

As soon as they were far enough away for Tasha not to see them, Wick shifted into his human form. His brothers shifted, too. "Fuck. What do we do now? Take off after those guys or stick with her? We can't leave her alone."

Paul rolled his shoulders, the moonlight showing his muscles. "We stick close to her, but we stay out of sight. Those must be the men who are after her mother. Looks to me like they're not planning on taking her alive. I sure as hell didn't like the weapons they carried. I wish like hell we could follow them, but I don't want to leave Tasha alone for long." He turned to his brother. "Shane, you run back to the house, get us some clothes, then hightail it back in the pickup. We can't help her get back to the house, but at least we can pick her up halfway home. We can always say we were out searching for her and lucked out running into her."

"Do you think that was her mother?" asked Shane. "If she was, why didn't she stick around to protect her daughter?"

"I don't know. But you're right. She shouldn't have run off." Wick suppressed the anger he felt toward the chupacabra. No real mother would've left her child—even a grown child—to face armed men alone.

"Maybe she took off thinking the men would chase after her." Shane shrugged. "We don't know enough to judge her."

Wick didn't want to agree. If he had it his way, he'd see Tasha's mother again and let her have it. "Whatever. We need to get moving. I think we scared those guys off, but we don't know that they won't come back. We've already left her alone and vulnerable long enough."

"Right. I'll get back as soon as I can." Shane shifted into his wolf then dashed off.

* * * *

Tasha felt like a damn idiot. Not only had she "borrowed" a horse—which had seemed like a good idea at the time—but then she'd lost that horse. Then, although she was grateful that the men had found her halfway back to the house and had given her a ride, she'd basically proven that she couldn't take care of herself.

But the men had been wonderful. They hadn't given her hell for taking the horse and had been more interested in finding out if she was all right. Had she been hurt after getting thrown from the horse? Did her feet hurt from the long walk? Did she have blisters? She'd done her best to make them understand that she was fine. And she was, except for her bruised ego. Thankfully, as she'd thought it would, the horse had found its way back to the barn.

The only time they'd given her any problem was when they'd refused to let her go into her camper. Instead, they'd insisted she come into the house and get something to eat. Until Shane had set the food in front of her, she hadn't realized how hungry she was. She'd eaten in silence, the men making small talk while they heaped more and more food on her plate.

At last, she'd had to push back from the table. "No more. I can't eat another bite. Thank you."

"Good," said Paul. "We like to see you eat."

His eyes brightened with bits of amber. She started to ask how that could happen, but now wasn't the time. She would've sworn the lust in his eyes said that he would love to eat her. Heat rose to her cheeks.

"Are you all right?" asked Wick.

It wasn't as though she could tell him the truth. "I'm fine. Really."

"Come on." Shane took her hand, bringing her along with him as he led the way into the living room.

"The dishes." She turned back, but he kept her moving.

"Don't worry about them. Wick will clean up later."

"I will?" From his surprised expression, Wick hadn't realized he was scheduled for clean-up duty. But he recovered nicely. "Sure, sure. I'll take care of it."

Tasha was exhausted, yet the strange, vibrant sensation she always felt around them was there yet again. Shane's touch had sent it into overdrive.

She studied the men, acknowledging how handsome they were, but knew the feeling didn't come from simple sexual attraction. Yes, it was very sexual, heating her from her pussy to travel throughout her limbs, but there was more to it than that. The electricity between them made her feel as though she'd known them for a lifetime.

No, that's not it.

It felt more like she'd been waiting for them her entire life. Waiting and wanting them without knowing they actually existed.

"We believe you."

Her gaze jumped to Paul. Was he joking? Maybe placating her? But, no, the truth was in his earnest expression. "You do?" She looked to the other men. "All of you?"

"I believe you, darlin'."

"We sure do," added Wick. "How can we doubt you when we saw it?" He cleared his throat. "I mean, her. Your mother."

"So you saw the chupacabra? You saw her?" Excitement rushed through her. To be believed renewed her strength. Yet, she had to tell them. "But I don't know if that was my mother. I didn't have time before—" She clammed up, unsure whether to tell them about the men.

"Before the men showed up." Paul sat on the edge of the couch, his expression intense. "Who were those guys? Do you have any idea?"

"I don't know who they are."

"But you've seen them before, haven't you?" pushed Wick. "You said as much, right?"

She nodded. "When I met my mother in the café and she told me everything, I saw them in the alley. But it was shadowed, and I didn't see their faces. And I didn't see them tonight, either. Did you?" But her hope was dashed at their silence.

"Damn. I was hoping you could give us a hint." Shane dropped his gaze to the floor as he grew deep in thought.

"So you saw my mother—I hope—and the men? But how? Where?" She stared at them, suddenly realizing they weren't being completely truthful with her. "You were there, weren't you?"

Again, the truth was written in their expressions and in their silence.

"I don't understand." She clenched her hands. She'd wanted to trust them, but how could she when they kept the truth from her? "You picked me up halfway back. If you were there, why didn't you help me? Why didn't you help my mother?"

Chapter Five

"We're busted, guys." Paul hadn't wanted Tasha to find out they'd been following her, but he wouldn't lie to her any longer. "Yes, Tasha, we were there."

Although she'd figured out what they'd done, she still didn't want to believe they'd lied to her. Hurt and disbelief were all too evident in her beautiful eyes. "You were there?"

Wick answered for them. "Yes. We were." He looked to Paul to explain.

Thanks for nothing. For once, I'd like one of them to take the lead.

But he had to keep going. Her searching look ate at him. "Yes, we followed you. We saw you taking off on the horse and didn't have any choice."

"Okay. I can understand what you must've been thinking, but I still don't get it. Since you were there, why wouldn't you help me?" She edged away from them. "I could've been hurt or killed, but you didn't show your faces. Why?"

What could he say? This time, he was the one to look to his brothers. If he stuck to telling her the truth, he'd have to tell her what they were. Was she ready? Or did she have enough problems to deal with?

Instead, he choked back the truth and forced another lie from his lips, forgoing his early vow not to lie again. "We got there late. By the time we found you, the men were leaving. The chupacabra left, too. All that was left was you and…"

Shit. I just fucked up.

"And the wolves." Her need to believe him, to trust him, flowed off her. "So you saw the three wolves and you still didn't step in to help me? This isn't making any sense. I thought I could trust you guys. I would've bet you'd help me if I needed it."

Paul's gut twisted. If he didn't start telling her the truth, he'd hate himself. "Look, Tasha, there's something you need to know."

She looked to him, eager for him to restore her faith in him. "Yes?"

Shane, however, knew what he was thinking and was ready to stop him from telling her they were werewolves. "We screwed up, darlin'. There's no other way to put it. We got there late, and then we just froze when we saw the wolves."

Shit. This is so fucking wrong.

It didn't matter who was doing the lying. They were all just as guilty. "Shane—"

But his brother wouldn't let him interrupt. He wouldn't let Paul tell the truth. "And then the wolves were gone. You weren't in any trouble any longer."

The quiet unnerved Paul even more. She looked to each of them, her confusion marring her sweet features.

"But why didn't you tell me you were there? Why didn't you take me home?" She shook her head. "Why wait to pick me up later? No. Nothing's making sense."

"We decided to let you walk home." Shane shot Paul a look silently asking for forgiveness. "Paul was still angry about you taking the horse without asking. He wanted to prove a point with you by letting you walk home. It was the wrong thing to do, and we're sorry as hell about it."

His brother had just thrown Paul under the bus. His wolf rose swiftly to the surface, growling, snarling, demanding to be set free to tear his brother apart. Wick's hand on Paul's shoulder, interrupting his anger, was the only thing that kept him from shifting.

Shane kept his attention diverted from Paul and centered on Tasha. He repeated the apology. "It was a shit move, and all of us are to blame. We screwed up, and we're sorry."

"So you let me walk all that way for nothing? But how'd you get there? I didn't hear the pickup."

"We'd parked away and followed you from there."

Paul gritted his teeth and kept his attention on the floor. When had his brother become such a liar? When had he?

"But how did you manage to follow me in a pickup? I went off the road and even backtracked. It was only luck that I found my mother. Or, actually, that she found me. And I sure don't know how those men found me, much less the wolves." She fell back against the couch. "I am so confused."

Paul checked with Shane then Wick. His look begged them for permission to tell her what they were. They'd promised each other that it would be a mutual decision to say when to tell their mate. He'd almost slipped up earlier, but he'd hold to that agreement now. Wick looked away, and a dejected-looking Shane barely shook his head.

Maybe they were right if they were thinking she had too much to handle already. His gut twisted even more. "When?" he silently asked, whispering so low that Tasha wouldn't hear him.

Instead of answering, Shane moved to sit next to Tasha. "I know. We messed up, and that's all there is to it. Believe me when I say we never wanted to do anything except make sure you were okay. Then, we even fucked that up. We were lucky in the end, but that doesn't make what we did any better." He slipped his arm around her shoulder.

Tears began to stream down Tasha's cheeks. Sobs wracked her body. Unable to stand it any longer, Paul got to his feet and pulled her against him.

"I'm sorry. Sorry for everything, sugar." He wrapped his arms around her as she clung to him, her sobs trembling against his chest, her tears wetting his shirt. "If there was any way to change things, I would."

"*We* would," added Wick. "Tasha, baby, we're going to make

things right. I swear we will."

"Damn straight." Shane stood, his expression filled with anguish. "We'll do everything we can to help you find your mother."

When she leaned away from Paul, he was stunned to see lust filling her eyes. The connection was stronger than ever, but he hadn't expected it to overrule the disappointment, the sorrow she had to be feeling.

"Can I stay here tonight?"

Had he heard her correctly? "Here? In the house?" He didn't want to assume anything. Not when they had so much to make up for.

She nodded, her tongue slipping between her lips. "Yes. Here. I don't want to be alone in my camper."

"Of course you can," answered an all-too-eager Wick. "You can stay here for the rest of your life."

She closed her eyes, and for one awful moment, Paul was certain Wick has said too much and frightened her off. Yet, when she reopened them, the need in her face had grown stronger. She looked toward the stairs, her meaning apparent.

Paul's wolf rose to the surface again, but this time for a completely different reason. Lifting her into his arms, he carried her to the stairs. She kept her attention focused on his face as Wick and Shane hurried past them.

* * * *

Was this really happening? Should she stop them? Yet, she wanted them more than she could put into words.

A door was opened.

Paul carried her into a huge bedroom. Slowly, carefully, he placed her on top of a massive bed. Carefully, reverently, the men surrounded her and began to undress her.

One by one, the pieces of her clothing were removed. With the toss of her shirt, the yank of her jeans, she kept her gaze moving from one man to the next. Once she was undressed, naked and vulnerable under their hot gazes, they stepped back and began to disrobe.

Her hunger rose as they revealed their magnificent bodies. Every tanned inch was perfection. They were beyond strong, their muscles rippling and flexing as they moved. They were rocks come to life, boulders set on top of other boulders made of soft, yet hard flesh. By the time they'd stripped, she could barely breathe.

"Ready, sugar?"

She couldn't answer. Instead, she closed her eyes. When his lips met hers, she drew in a breath then began savoring the roughness of Paul's masculine lips against hers. At first, the kiss was tentative as though asking permission, a permission he didn't need. Still, after what the men had done, following her then not helping her, they had to feel hesitant to demand anything from her. Yet, although she knew she should be angry, the sensation whipping into a frenzy inside her wouldn't let her push them away. She needed them as much as she needed the air to breathe.

The kiss grew in intensity, deepening as his tongue savagely plunged inside to play a game of chase with hers. She played the game, toying with his tongue, only to offer hers to him again. His was a unique mixture of flavors, and she savored them all.

Suddenly, Paul broke the kiss to travel his mouth down to her nipples. He tortured them, sucking, nibbling, tugging until she squirmed with need.

Had Shane and Wick gone? She'd no sooner thought the question then it was answered.

Shane fell next to her and eased her onto her side. His hands played with her butt cheeks as Paul continued to ravish her hardened nipples. She was consumed with a fiery need and reached for both the men, determined to force them to give her their cocks. If they didn't fuck her and soon, she'd go crazy.

Wick eased between her legs then slid his hand along her hip to find its way over the inside of her thigh to between her legs. "Are you wet yet, baby? If not, I'm going to make you wet. I want to feel your juices on my fingers."

As if he didn't already know she was wet. Couldn't he see the moisture? Couldn't he smell her arousal? How could he not know when he'd already eased a finger between her folds and dipped it into her pussy?

"You're wet as all get-out, baby. This is exactly what I needed." He pulled his finger out and sucked her juices from it. "Juicy and sweet, just like I knew you'd be."

"Please." Her body purred from their caresses, their words of lust. They made promises of a forever she wanted to believe in, but couldn't.

Not yet. Maybe later. Think about it later.

"No need to ask. We're going to give you everything you need or want." Wick grabbed her behind the legs and pulled her closer. With a wicked grin, he lay between her legs.

She gasped as his tongue found her clit and swept over it. "Oh God, yes. Please. Suck harder."

Paul took her chin then kissed her again. A sweep of his tongue skimmed along the seam of her mouth. "You're the only thing that matters to us. I swear we'll prove it to you."

Their touches were sweet, but his words were even sweeter. She fought back the urge to cry again. "Just make love to me."

Not sex. Love. Because this is so much more than sex.

The idea frightened her as much as it thrilled her.

"Hey, baby, are you all right?" Wick lifted up, her juices surrounding his mouth.

"I'm fine." She was better than fine.

Then Wick went back to her pussy, sending trembles through her. Paul bit at a nipple, giving her a bite of pain that was followed by a rush of craving to have him bite her again.

"First things first. I want a taste of what Wick's getting. You sure look good, sugar. Sweet as hell." Paul shoved Wick aside then laid his upper torso over her leg and put his mouth to her pussy.

Spreading her legs wider, she gave herself to him. His tongue plundered her pussy, sweeping over her clit to dive into her entrance. The noises he made were thrilling, causing her to grow even wetter. He sucked on her clit then ran his tongue on the inside of her folds.

Heat, primal and unyielding, burned inside her. The strange feeling had grown so powerful that she could no longer think. Instead, she was all body, all senses, without a mind to tell her that what she was doing was risky. The men talked of a future, yet, unlike her body, she couldn't commit her mind to that promise.

Not yet. Maybe later.

Shane shoved Paul away. "My turn to get a taste."

She'd barely had time to register what he'd said before Shane had his mouth on her. He captured her clit with his teeth and sucked, adding a delightful pain to the already overwhelming sensations spinning her out of control.

Wick moved beside her and took her breasts in his hands. "You're beautiful. You know that, don't you? Or don't you? You should because every damn inch of you is beyond amazing."

Bending over, he took her nipple into his mouth. He worked his teeth back and forth, sending swift stabs of pain into her breasts. The pain, however, didn't hurt much. Instead, it had her head spinning, her lust building even higher.

"Here, sugar. Take my dick."

She opened her mouth, accepting Paul's huge cock dripping with pre-cum. Sucking, she let his juices sing in her mouth.

Shane urged her on. "Damn, but you're one sexy woman. That's it, darlin', suck on him hard. Hollow your cheeks. Drain him dry."

She cupped Wick's balls, loving the weight against her palm. He groaned when she wrapped her hand around his length. He played with her tits as she worked him, pulling, tugging as she lashed Paul's cock with her tongue.

"Enough. I have to have her." Paul moved to settle between her legs, shoving Shane away. Shane's mouth lifted into a snarl that reminded her of the way the black wolf had snarled.

For a moment, only a moment, fear took her. But when Paul pulled her legs around his waist, she forgot all about the animal. She had three animal-like men in bed with her.

She took Wick's cock in and compared his taste to Paul's. He tasted different, yet he had that same underlying wildness she couldn't define. He caught her breasts and fondled them, at first gently and lovingly then roughly, his thumbs raking over her nipples.

She hadn't realized it before, but they treated her as all women wanted to be treated. Roughly, yet with respect and caring. She surrendered to them, not as a weak woman but because she was strong enough to let them be in charge.

Their hands worked magic on her as their hard, sexy bodies spread their heat along her skin. She cried out as an orgasm surged outward, stunning her with its arrival.

Paul pounded into her, his rough grunts adding to her lust. Her own grunts echoed his. His eyes, dotted more with the strange amber color, locked onto hers. "You're mine. Ours. Remember that." Then, with one last plunge, he drove his cock as far into her as was physically possible. He stilled, his body stiffening. Then, all at once, he groaned and turned his release free.

Warmth filled her as his cum shot inside her. She clenched her pussy muscles, doing her best to hold his seed inside her.

But why would she want that? Why hadn't she demanded condoms? Yet the why didn't matter. The answer was somewhere deep inside her, and she trusted that answer.

"Come here, sugar."

Paul fell to the side as Wick shoved him away. Before she could think, Wick plunged his cock inside her pussy.

"Fuck me, baby. Fuck me hard." Taking hold of her legs, he spread them wide and hooked them over his elbows. Then, with bits of amber sparking in his eyes, he drove his cock deep inside her again and again.

She yelped as he entered her, forcing her pussy walls to give way to his massive length and width. He filled her, impossibly pushing her walls to their limit.

Another orgasm built inside her, its whirling need spinning until she was certain she'd black out. Shane and Paul came to each side of her, each taking a breast. While they massaged her tits and sucked on her nipples, Wick shoved into her time and again, harder and harder.

She screamed as the second climax tore her apart. Her body shuddered under the onslaught, yet Wick continued to plunge harder, deeper.

"On your side, darlin'. I'm tired of waiting for my turn." Shane eased her back onto her side even as his fingers found her dark hole and began to persuade her to give way to them.

What about lubrication? Yet, she didn't voice her question. Even after they'd let her down, she still trusted them. Even in this.

Shane put his cock to her anus then leaned over so he could look into her eyes. "This won't hurt much after the first little bit. You believe that, don't you?"

She nodded. She couldn't do much more.

When he entered her, sliding into her at the same time Wick thrust his cock again into her pussy, she sucked in a hard breath. The men pounded into her, setting up a rhythm. She joined them physically, but it was the odd sensation that really joined them. Even with Paul watching silently to the side, he was still a part of their union. She reached out a hand to him, needing to touch him.

Together, the four of them became one.

Wick shoved one last time into her then paused. She felt him stiffen a moment before he laid back his head and growled his release. Hot cum shot into her.

It wasn't a minute later that Shane tensed, made a strangled sound, then shoved into her again. In the same moment Wick pulled out, Shane did, as well. Warm seed struck her lower back.

Her third—*third!*—orgasm came quickly, overtaking her, sending her mind reeling. She cried out, her body coming apart.

By the time she could think straight again, the men were already telling her how much they wanted her, how long they'd waited for her. Although she didn't understand some of what they said, she loved hearing them talk about her and the life they wanted with her.

"It's the feeling you're getting, sugar. That's what we call the connection. It's a special bond that joins men and the woman they're intended to mate."

She snuggled against Shane with Wick and Paul nearby. "Your mate? That's like being your wife, right?"

"Yeah. It's the same thing."

Wick played with her nipple, and she slapped his hand away. She needed to think, and if he didn't stop teasing her, she'd forget everything else except the desire coming to life again.

"And you're saying we're meant for each other? So it's like love at first sight?" She wouldn't have believed such a thing was possible. Yet since she'd learned about chupacabras, she could believe in most anything.

"That's right." Paul caressed her cheek. "We know this is hard to take in, but what we're telling you is the truth. We knew from the first moment we saw you that you were the one for us." His dark eyes beckoned to her. "And we're pretty sure you knew the same thing. Are we right?"

"I don't know. I definitely felt that weird pull toward you three. Something kept making me want to beg you to take me." She twisted to look into his face, those eyes. "I've never experienced anything like it before. In fact, I feel it right now."

"So do you want to stay with us?" asked Wick, almost timidly. "Forever, I mean. Not just until you find your mother."

The mention of her mother gave her a sinking feeling. "If it weren't for my mother, I'd say yes right away. As it is, I'm not sure if I can promise anything."

"Then we need to find her as soon as possible," said Shane. "She's a chupacabra, and I'm willing to bet she's the one we saw. All we need to do is to find her."

"Yeah. That's all." Tasha chuckled, but sarcasm dripped from her tone. "And we need to do it before those men kill her."

"Do you think they want to kill her?" asked Paul. "Maybe they want to do the same thing you're trying to do. Maybe they want to take her alive."

She sat up, suddenly anxious that they didn't truly understand. "I'm not trying to capture her. I'm trying to save her life. She gave me the tracking device so I could find her dead body. I'd rather find her live one instead." Easing away from them, she asked the most important question of all. "Will you help me find her or not?"

* * * *

"We didn't tell her everything." Wick threw a saddle on top of Ranger. He kept his voice low, not wanting Tasha to hear in case she came into the barn sooner than he expected. "Basically, we're lying to her again."

"We're not lying," professed Shane. "We're just not telling her what we are yet. We need to take this one thing at a time. Once we make sure her mother is safe, then we'll tell her about us."

Wick sent a questioning look to Paul, but Paul was keeping silent. "Fine. But as soon as this thing with her mother is settled, we tell her. No ifs, ands, or buts. Agreed?"

"Agreed," answered Shane.

Paul remained silent, but his silence was his agreement.

* * * *

Tasha squirmed in her seat. The men had promised that her horse Bloomer was one of the gentler animals, but that didn't make the saddle any softer. They'd been riding for a few hours after the sun had set, and she was getting worried that, once again, they wouldn't find her mother. After three nights of searching, she'd expected to run into her at least once.

Worry continued to plague her. Was she too late? Had the men, whoever they were, gotten to her mother first?

"Don't worry," said Paul as though he could read her mind. "We'll find her." He checked the tracking device he held.

"It's almost sunrise. We won't be able to look much longer." At least she'd figured out that the chupacabra was a nocturnal animal.

They'd searched for the past three nights, going back to the ranch at daybreak to fall exhausted into the huge bed they'd said they'd saved for their mate. As soon as they woke up later in the day, they made love and talked about what it meant for her to become their mate. Fortunately, they wanted a large family like she did. Fortunately, she was willing, even happy, to move to Forever and live on their ranch. The longer she stayed there, the more she loved the land. Soon, they'd take her into Forever and introduce her to their friends.

The beeping of the tracking device caught their attention. She leaned forward, trying to see yet knowing she was too far from Paul to get a good look.

"She's close. Real close." Paul's voice was filled with excitement. "And heading in our direction. Get ready."

When the dark form raced past her as had happened before, she was prepared. Her horse danced, excited, but she managed to keep it under control.

"Follow us, sugar," shouted Paul as he let his mount break into a run. Wick grinned at her as he took off after his brother. Shane waited expectantly for her to get her horse moving.

She held on as Bloomer broke into a run. Shane let out a shout and raced past her. If she wasn't chasing after her elusive mother, she would've loved having the wind in her hair, loved the feel of the powerful animal between her legs. As it was, though, she set her sights on keeping up with the men.

They raced over the landscape. She caught glimpses of the chupacabra as it darted in and out of the bushes. But it was fast, faster than the horses. A knot formed in her throat, fear trying to take hold. Running a horse over the rugged land was perilous during the daytime, but at night, it was even more terrifying. Yet the men were willing to put their horses and themselves in danger to help her mother. How could she do any less?

Paul and Wick disappeared around a bend in the hard-packed dirt road. She nudged her horse with her heels again, encouraging it to keep up with Shane's horse that was slightly ahead of hers. Taking the turn by leaning into it and hanging on for her life, Tasha was propelled into a clearing. She pulled on the reins, bringing the horse to a sudden stop. Bloomer nickered, protesting and sending dirt flying as he dug his hooves into the ground.

Tasha's heart leapt to her throat. Fear locked onto her as she clung to the horse's saddle.

No. Please, no.

A gunshot blasted the air.

Chapter Six

Shane pushed his horse to the limit, trying to catch up with his brothers, praying that his mount wouldn't lose its footing and send them both crashing to the ground. If it did, he'd end up trapped under the weight of the animal. But he had to keep up.

By the time he'd eaten up some of the distance between them, he'd taken the curve in the road, leaning along with his horse to make the sharp turn. Shane was as startled as Tasha and his brothers. "Shit."

Paul and Wick dismounted, turning their horses free to skitter away. Their eyes burned with amber as they tore their clothes from their bodies. Shane wanted to tell them to stop, to stay human, but knew they were right in what they did. Although Paul had brought his rifle, it would be of little use now.

His attention went to the two men dressed in black. The men stood over the body of the chupacabra but still had their guns pointed at the animal.

The men put their attention squarely on Paul and Wick as they went through their transformations. One man said something to the other. They both lifted their rifles to aim at his brothers.

"Shane? Oh God. Shane."

Shane slipped off his horse, gave the animal a hard pat on its rump and sent it after his brothers' horses. "Tasha, listen to me."

She stared at the animal on the ground, her gaze fixed, her eyes shining. Was she in shock? Did she even see the men and her brothers?

"Tasha?" He spoke softly even as his brothers' growls filled the air, their changes complete. Striding over to her, he put a hand on her leg. "Come to me," he ordered, hoping his stern voice could break through her shock.

She blinked then looked down at him, confusion unable to mar her beautiful face. "Shane?" she asked, as though she hadn't realized he was there.

He held open his arms and kept his gaze with hers. "Come to me, darlin'. Keep your eyes on me and slide into my arms."

The growls grew louder, now accompanied by shouts and then— to Shane's horror—a gunshot.

Tasha jerked away from him at the report of the gun. Her attention swung back to the animal lying on the ground. Slowly, she turned her head to the scene several feet away. Her mouth parted, and she blinked yet again.

Shane glanced to where she was looking. Paul and Wick, now fully in werewolf forms, stood over the bodies of the two men. Blood ran down Paul's right leg, but Shane doubted it was more than a flesh wound. Paul's werewolf healing properties would take care of the wound quickly enough.

He twisted back to Tasha. "Get off the horse, darlin'. Please."

The wild look in her eyes was enough to frighten him. That, along with the trembling that racked her body, terrified him. He couldn't wait for her to respond. Instead, he grabbed her arm and pulled her to him.

She fell into his arms then fought against him, putting her hands against his chest to push away. "No. Leave her alone." Pulling her tranquilizer gun from its saddle holster, she darted toward his brothers.

Shane snagged her arm as she lifted the rifle to her shoulder. "No, don't."

She tried to pull out of his hold but couldn't. "Kill them. We have to kill them. It's my mother. It has to be her. We have to help her."

Shane locked his arms around her from behind, holding her while keeping her from lifting the gun again. He tightened his hold until, at last, she had no choice but to drop the weapon.

"Noooo. We have to kill them."

Paul and Wick lowered their bodies to the ground, hoping to make themselves look less threatening. They kept their ears forward and their tails wagging side by side, true signs that they were friendly.

"Darlin', try to calm down." She hadn't mentioned seeing his brothers change, but how could she have missed it?

She dragged in several deep breaths, the trembling slowly subsiding. "Turn me free, Shane."

He was hesitant to do so. "Are you all right?"

She craned her neck around to glare at him. "Turn me free."

He did, releasing her slowly, gently. As soon as he wasn't touching her any longer, she dashed toward the chupacabra. Falling to her knees, she bent over the animal then put a hand to its head. "Mom? Is it you? Mom, please answer me. Please come back to me."

Shane came up behind her but didn't touch her. He'd let her have her time, giving her the chance to say good-bye. If the animal wasn't her mother, they'd keep looking. But if it was, then they'd be there for her.

The chupacabra moved. It was a slight movement, but enough to show it was still alive. Its eyes opened and stared up at Tasha.

"Mom?"

"Be careful, Tasha. It might not be your mother." He stood at the ready in case the animal tried to bite her.

"Mom, please come back to me," she begged.

Shane was almost certain the animal wasn't Tasha's mother, but when he noticed her form growing blurry and heard the snap of its bones changing, he knew he was wrong.

Wary, Tasha eased back as the animal shifted. Soon, a woman who looked like an older version of Tasha lay on the ground.

* * * *

It can't be. This is not my mother.

Yet, as much as she hoped she was right, she had to face the facts as the chupacabra changed into a woman. A sob broke from Tasha as she pulled her mother onto her lap.

"Mom? Mom, just stay calm. We're going to get you help. I promise."

Promise. Hadn't the men promised her they'd help find her mother? But they'd been too late.

"Honey?" Her mother's voice was only a whisper.

"Yeah, Mom. I'm here." Tasha wiped a tear away. "Don't talk. Save your strength." At last, she turned toward Shane. "Call someone, please. Get her help." Her gaze flitted to the two wolves sitting next to her mother's hunters. She darted her gaze back to her mother, unwilling and unable to handle anything more than taking care of her mother.

Not now. Maybe later.

"Honey, it's okay." Blood trickled from her mother's mouth and down her chin.

"Please, Mom."

Please what? Don't die? Don't let the wound in your chest bleed all over my legs?

"I'm sorry I wasn't a better mother." Her mother stopped, her face scrunching in pain, her eyes closing. When she opened her eyes again, they were dotted with red. Was it the red of the chupacabra's eyes? Or was it blood?

"It doesn't matter now. All that matters is that you stay alive. Please. Don't leave me." *Not again.*

Her mother managed a weak smile. "I love you, honey. Through it all, I always loved you."

She never would've believed she'd hear those words ever again. Never would've believed she'd say them to her mother. "I love you, too, Mommy."

Her mother attempted to lift a hand to touch her. Tasha took hold of her mother's hand and lifted it for her, placing it against her cheek. "Please, don't die."

"Are they dead?"

Tasha didn't want to talk about the hunters. "They can't hurt you now. But, Mom, please don't talk. Save your strength."

"I have to tell you. They wanted me dead." Her mother managed a weak smile. "Looks like they're going to get what they wanted."

"But why?"

Her mother groaned, closing her eyes against the pain. "Because I dared to love them."

Tasha's mind whirled. "What? I don't understand."

"I loved them both. And they loved me. But that was before"—her mother groaned again—"I was bitten. Before I became something they couldn't love. When they found out, they couldn't stand the idea of being involved with an animal. I tried to leave, but that wasn't enough. They wanted me gone forever. Erased as though I never existed."

Tasha glanced at the dead men. Their bodies were bloodied and torn, but she felt no sympathy. She shook her head, silently asking her mother to keep quiet. "Hang on. We're going to get you help."

"It's too late." Again, her mother closed her eyes against the pain. When she opened them, she looked to Shane. "I should never have involved her. Don't tell anyone about them. Get rid of their bodies. Get rid of mine."

"No. You're going to be all right. You have to be." Tears wet her face. How could she bear to lose her mother yet again?

The pain shone in her mother's eyes. "I'm sorry, honey."

"No. Mom, don't."

Her mother drew in a ragged breath then slowly exhaled it.

Tasha stared at her mother, willing her to take another breath. Yet she knew she wouldn't. She was gone. "Nooo!" she wailed. "Please, come back. Mommy, come back." She'd said the same words so many years earlier and never thought she'd say them again.

Shane took her by the arms. "Darlin', let me take care of her. Come on. Let's get you back to the ranch."

Pain turned into an ugly anger. "You promised you'd find her." She kept her attention glued to her mother as she gently eased her off her lap and onto the ground. "You promised."

"I'm sorry. We tried, but we were too late."

The pain erupted into even more anger. Shoving him away, she staggered to her feet and whirled on him. "Get away from me!" She pointed at him then switched to pointing at the two wolves. "All of you just stay the fuck away from me!"

"Darlin'—"

"Shut up!" Tears burned in her eyes and blurred her vision. "You lied to me. You promised you'd find her." She pulled her lips back into a snarl. "You're nothing but animals! I know what you are. You're fucking werewolves." Her focus shifted back to Shane, unsure, but assuming he was like his brothers. "All of you."

"Let us explain."

But she had no intention of listening to Shane, to any of them. "No. Leave me alone."

Still, she couldn't help but stare as the two wolves began to change, their forms blurring as her mother's had. Soon enough, they were back in their human forms. "You're werewolves." If she said the words enough times, would believing become easier?

Paul and Wick moved toward her then stopped at her glare. "It's true, sugar. We're werewolves. How'd you know?"

She snorted her derision. "I didn't. Not until you changed. But it doesn't take a fucking genius to figure it out. My mother was a shifter. Once I saw you change and attack those men, I knew."

"Well, at least we don't have figure out how to tell her now."

Paul and Shane glared at Wick. "Now's not the time for jokes, man," said Paul. He took a few more steps closer. "Sugar, you're probably still in shock. Let's round up the horses and get you back home."

She rushed to snatch up the tranquilizer gun. Raising it, she pointed it at Paul. "Stay back. Stay the hell back or I'll shoot you. I swear I will."

"You don't mean that," said Shane as he moved toward her, too. "We won't hurt you. You know that. We love you. You're our mate."

"Mate." She laughed. "Now the word makes sense. I'm supposed to be your mate. I'm supposed to be your bitch."

Anger flared in Paul's eyes, amber bits highlighting them. Their eyes had been full of amber as wolves. "Your eyes. I always meant to ask you. Your eyes get amber in them because you're werewolves."

"When our wolf comes closer to the surface, then, yes, our eyes fill with amber," answered Wick.

"You promised to find my mother." She risked a look at her mother, felt the terrible stab of grief, then motioned at Shane. "Take off your shirt. She deserves more than to lie there naked."

He stripped off his shirt then walked over and covered her mother's torso with it. "We'll take her home with us and give her a decent burial."

"No. She told you what to do. You'd better damn well do it."

"Whatever you want, baby."

Her mother had known it would end up with her death. Tasha, however, had dared to think she could save her. She couldn't get the refrain out of her head. "You promised to find her."

"We did. And we kept that promise." Paul shook his head. "I'm sorry we didn't keep the promise in time."

Suddenly, looking at her mother again, the anger fell away, eroded by the overwhelming pain. "She's dead."

They were with her then, taking the gun away as they pulled her into a circle of their comfort. She moaned then, unable to hold it back any longer, turned the sobs free.

"It's going to be okay, baby," said Wick. "We'll take care of everything."

Paul pulled her close, wrapping his strong arms around her. "Let it out, sugar. Let it out."

She did, crying harder than she'd ever cried before. "She's gone. I loved her, and now she's gone." Every ounce of strength fled her. Her legs buckled, and she felt herself falling.

Paul lifted her into his arms. "Let's go home."

* * * *

Tasha drew in the smell of the rose bush the men had planted along the railing of the house. She smiled, remembering how they'd argued over the best way to plant the bushes.

Her mother had loved roses. That was one of the few things she remembered about her mother from her childhood. Strange how she'd started remembering good memories of her mother. Perhaps her mother hadn't been a good parent, but maybe she'd tried her best. At least, in the end, they'd managed to come together.

A month later and the memory of her mother's death still hurt almost as much as it had that night they'd found her. Fulfilling her mother's last wishes, she and the men had burned her body. They'd buried her ashes under a huge tree near the house so Tasha could visit her whenever she wanted. The men had taken the killers' bodies somewhere else. Tasha hadn't asked what they'd done with the bodies and she vowed she never would.

Telling her brothers that their mother was dead had been difficult, especially when she'd had to lie and tell them a fever had taken her. Uncaring, they hadn't questioned her story.

Through it all, the men had handled everything, allowing her to mourn in peace. Through it all, they'd given her the time and space she'd needed to accept them for what they were. But she'd had enough time. The time for mourning was over. Now she wanted to begin her future.

Wick and Shane were busy arguing over how to get the pickup running again. As she'd seen time and time again, Paul would cast the deciding vote. Whoever was right, however, would razz the others to no end. Or, at least, until the next argument started.

She tilted her head to the side and studied her men. They'd given her so much without asking anything in return. Not only had they taken care of her mother's body but they'd supported her when she'd made the decision to turn the leave of absence she'd taken from her job into a permanent situation. At one point, they'd even offered to do a long-distance romance until they could sell the ranch and move to the city. But she'd known they would've been miserable with all the noise and people. Besides, she'd fallen in love not only with the men but with the ranch.

It's time.

She stood up and walked to the end of the porch. "Hey, guys?"

Shane jolted upward, bumping his head on the open hood of the truck. "Shit."

Wick laughed as he turned his attention to her. His dark eyes sparkled just as they did every time he looked at her.

Paul stopped pounding a nail into the corral, a similar gleam in his eyes. "Yeah?"

"You guys have been really good to me."

Wick frowned at her, confused. "What else would we be but good to you? You're our mate."

Wasn't she more? Yet had they ever told her that they loved her? Had she told them? It seemed she'd let a lot of things slide while she'd mourned her mother.

"I mean more than good. You helped me get through an awful time, and you didn't push me."

Paul put the hammer down and sauntered over to his brothers. "I feel like you're getting at something. So how about you just get to it?"

At times, Paul could seem a little harsh, but she'd learned that he had a soft heart. His brothers had the same sweetness about them, hidden ever so carefully under their rugged exteriors. Even when they shifted into their wolf forms, they were sweet and loving, almost puppy-like at times.

"Okay. I will." She tugged her T-shirt over her head and flung it away. That got their attention in a major way. Her shorts, along with her panties, found the hardwood beneath her.

"Damn," said Wick. "Talk about getting to it."

"An understatement if ever I heard one," added Paul.

Shane licked his lips. "I think I know what you're trying to tell us."

She smiled, loving the hunger on their faces. "You know part of it."

"What's the rest of it?" asked Wick. "Tell me before I can't think straight."

"Okay. Here it is." She drew in a breath, knowing the next words would change her life forever. "I love you."

There. She'd said it, and it was way overdue.

They seemed astonished at first, their eyes widening. Then came the smiles followed by the simmering heat of the connection roaring into a blazing fire, amber dotting their eyes. They started toward her.

"Come here, darlin'." Shane grabbed hold of her and pressed a hard kiss to her lips.

She could hear the sounds of the other two men hurriedly getting naked. Smiling into the kiss, she worked at Shane's belt buckle, but her fingers were suddenly useless.

Their hands skimmed over her body, caressing her with their words of need first, followed swiftly by words filled with love that warmed her heart. The connection never left her completely any longer, but it whipped into a greater frenzy after being so long without their touch to thrill her.

"Bed," demanded Paul.

She shook her head. "I can't wait that long. Here. Now."

"Then I have to taste you, sugar."

"Then taste me."

"Don't take long. I want my cock inside her," answered Shane as he worked his hand between them and massaged a nipple.

"What are we waiting for, guys? Use the swing. Use whatever," added an impatient Wick, whose eyes were flecked with amber.

Paul lifted her off her feet, carried her to the swing they'd put on the porch just for her. He dropped to his knees in front of her then leaned forward, a starving man ready for his first meal. She gasped as he put his mouth against her pussy.

Wick sat on the swing beside her and took her breasts in his hands. As his tongue tortured one nipple, his thumb raked over the other.

Shane went behind the swing. He took her by the chin and eased her head back. She saw his hungry face for a moment before he pressed a kiss to her mouth. It had been far too long since she'd tasted his flavors, and she pulled his tongue inside, eagerly tasting them.

Paul's tongue was a weapon of seduction as he lapped up her juices. His tongue pierced her pussy while his thumb changed her clit into a throbbing mass of muscles that might melt under the heat of his touch. When he put his teeth to her clit then thrust two fingers into her sheath, she cried out, but her cry was smothered by Shane's passionate kiss.

The brothers were alike yet uniquely different in the way they made love. Paul was serious, steadily working her clit and her pussy until every inch of her hummed under his masterful attention. Wick whispered terms of endearment in her ear, at once turning her on then making her inwardly giggle. Shane wasn't about to be outdone and intensified his kiss, including nibbles to her lips.

She reached out to take Wick's cock, but he pushed her hand aside. "Nah, baby. Just lie back and enjoy."

She broke the kiss she shared with Shane and earned an unhappy growl from him. "But I want to taste you." She batted her eyelashes at Wick then flicked her tongue over her upper lip, tempting him. He groaned, at once giving in. Standing, he put his foot on the swing and offered her his cock.

She drew him in, loving the difference in flavors between Shane's mouth and Wick's cock. Not that she'd ever talk about it with them. They'd probably end up arguing about which one tasted better. She smiled as she rounded her mouth around his length. She would, of course, be the judge.

Shane bent over the back of the swing, his hands cupping her breasts as he kissed, fondled, pinched, and nibbled the curve of her neck, the slope of her shoulders. She whimpered as her body heated up even more, firing the connection to full force.

She inhaled as Paul flattened his tongue against her clit and showed her how easily he could command her body. Cupping Wick's balls, she used the other hand to grab a hunk of Paul's hair, holding him to her pussy.

If anyone had stopped by, she wouldn't have cared. Nothing on earth would make her break free of them.

Wick pulled his cock back all too soon. When she cast an irritation look his way, he explained, "If I don't, I'm going to blow too soon."

"I could drink you up," she replied, knowing how it would get to him. When he closed his eyes and groaned, she knew she had.

"No, baby. Not today. It's been too long since I've had my cock inside you."

"Same here." Paul wiped her juices from his mouth then stood. He took one of her legs, forcing her to turn on her side. Wrapping the chain of the chair around a planter hook on the house, he kept the swing as still as he could. Then, kneeling in such a way that only a powerful man could do, he positioned his cock at her pussy and plunged it inside.

She let out a cry that was short-lived. Paul set his hips into motion, thrusting his cock again and again into her pussy. The swing rocked back and forth in short moves with each thrust, yet was held steadier as it was caught between the men. Paul's chest was wide and muscled, a rock shelf she longed to climb. Yet the only thing she could manage to do right then was to skim her fingers along the soft-hardness.

Her breasts bounced prettily until Wick covered them with his hands. "Better get it done fast, man. I'm not going to wait much longer."

"I second that," added Shane as he moved to sit beside her, adding his weight to keep the rocking of the swing to a minimum. "In fact…"

Without warning, Shane lifted her up, taking her away from both of his brothers. They snarled, their wolves angry and rising to the surface, but Shane only laughed. His laughter, however, turned into a satisfied groan as he brought her down on top of his lap.

Shane's eyes met hers as his cock pushed into her pussy. "Damn, how I need you."

Tasha gripped his shoulders, hanging on as he drove into her, riding her up and down. His cock pushed the limits of her pussy, setting up a delicious friction that made the burn inside her hotter. The storm inside her built higher, too, driving to its culmination. Closing her eyes, she let the fiery whirlwind take her, sending her flying as the orgasm burst free.

Shane gripped the back of her neck. "Open your eyes. I want to see you come."

She did as he'd ordered and saw his own release strike him. Tensing, he kissed her hard then drove into her one last time. His growl flowed into her mouth as he shot his cum into her. Clinging together, they forgot the other men existed.

At least until Paul lifted her away from Shane. "I'm taking her back, you ass." His chuckle warmed her shoulder as he wrapped his arms around her. "Speaking of ass…"

"And pussy, damn it." Wick shoved a slumped Shane out of the swing. "Give her to me."

"Fine. Don't tell you I never gave you anything."

She spread wide as Paul placed her onto Wick's lap. "Funny, guys. Real—" The last word was lost as Wick took her by the neck and pulled her mouth to his. His kiss was needy, urgent, and captured her cry as his cock drove into her pussy.

Paul's hand on her back eased her forward. His fingers played with her dark hole, preparing her, working her tight muscles. Thankfully, lube wasn't needed with werewolves. That was just one of the many things she'd come to love about their alter-selves.

The swing swayed as Paul slipped his cock into her asshole. Gripping Wick's shoulders, she pushed against him even as he shoved his hips forward, driving his cock deeper. Amber flared in his eyes, and not for the first time, she wondered what it would be like to be a female werewolf and make love to their animals.

Shane watched, speaking to her again of love and fidelity, of the life they would share. He spoke for all three men, telling her how lucky they were to have found her. She wanted to tell them she was the lucky one but couldn't find the breath, much less the words, as Paul and Wick rammed into her, capturing not only her body but her heart between them. They'd brought her wild side to life, yet she wanted them to bring another, even wilder side of her to life.

Soon, I'll tell them. Not later. Soon.

The three of them moved together like a well-oiled machine, each giving, each taking. The storm that had already come to shore once rose up again, doubling then tripling in intensity. She arched her back, giving Wick her breasts to ravish, her ass cheeks for Paul to keep her steady.

"You're our mate, now and forever," said Paul in a tense voice.

"I am. And you're mine. All of you. I love you." She'd barely gotten the words out between gasps for air.

They spoke at once, almost simultaneously declaring their love for her.

"We love you, too, baby."

"We all love you, darlin'."

Paul's breath warmed her ear. "I love you. We love you. Never forget."

How could she ever forget? Joy filled her.

Suddenly, Shane grabbed her by the hair. "Do you want to become one of us? It's your choice. Do you?"

She'd thought about being changed often enough to have come to a decision before today. "Yes. Change me."

Soon had come sooner than she'd imagined it would.

"Now?" asked Wick.

"Yes. Now."

"Are you sure?" asked Shane. "It's not an easy thing to go through."

She didn't care. Whatever she had to endure would be worth it. The storm swirled, moving faster, ready to obliterate her. "Do it now." Her orgasm threatened to take the ability to speak from her. "Now!"

Fangs erupted from Wick's mouth as he cupped her neck again and put his teeth to her skin. As his fangs sank into her flesh, her climax broke free. She screamed, more from the release than from the pain searing into her neck. The world spun around her as Paul and Wick gave freedom to their climaxes.

* * * *

I have to run harder, faster.

The thought wasn't like a thought would be while Tasha was in her human body. They weren't comprised of words but consisted more of emotions, sensations, and feelings no human words could ever hope to describe.

Tasha's tongue lolled from her mouth as her feet dug into the dirt. The wind blew through her fur as she lengthened her stride, determined to keep pace with the men.

They'd told the truth about the transformation. For two days, she'd been deathly ill, certain she'd die. At times, even wishing she'd die. Yet they'd stayed by her side, reassuring her, telling her how much they loved her.

She'd wanted to run with them the minute she'd started feeling better. Together, they'd guided her through her first shift, and now, three days later, she was an old pro at it. Of course, it still hurt, but the end result was well worth it. They'd unleashed her wild side, and she was thrilled that they had.

She ran faster, getting even with the other three wolves. Glancing at the full moon above them, she smiled a wolfish smile.

Home.

Once they made it home, she'd take them to bed and show them her real wild side.

THE END

WWW.JANEJAMISON.COM

Siren Publishing, Inc.
www.SirenPublishing.com

Lightning Source UK Ltd.
Milton Keynes UK
UKHW02f2100220218
318351UK00011BA/704/P

9 781642 430226